Ginny
The Continuing Adventures
of a Young Cowboy

Stu Campbell

ISBN: 978-0-9962019-5-7

6   5   4   3   2   1

Edited by Mira Perrizo
Cover and text design by D.K. Luraas
Cover painting by Larry Jones, Bouse, Arizona

Printed in the United States of America

Contents

Something Amiss

Things seemed to be going well at the Wilson Ranch and I was pleased. There was plenty of grass, a good calf crop was on the ground, most all of the mares had good paint colts at their sides, and the cabins were booked full for the summer. Two new cabins had been added and the ranch now had the capacity to house sixty people, perhaps a few more if the kids were added. Bud was spending the winters in town in the house Sally had designed and built, and he came out to the ranch for the summers, as did Missus Abercrombie, Sally, and Ginny. Ginny had started kindergarten and Sally wanted to make sure she had a good opportunity for a proper education, a fact that I was sure Missus Abercrombie had weighed in on a great deal.

The crew consisted of Pat and Chuck, two full-time year-round employees, the cook, and four wranglers—Jimmy McIntyre, who had worked on the Wilson Ranch for a number of years, and Devin, Blake, and Quince, college students hired for the summer. Sally and Bud had gone to the college and hired them along with some girls to do the maid work. They had also hired an assistant cook, Walter, to help out in the kitchen, hoping to hire him year round as the cook was starting to show his age and slowing down. And, of course, my sister Betty came to help with Ginny. All and all there were about sixteen employees for the summer, not counting me.

I'm Honey. The nickname was put on me a few years ago before Sally and I were married. I didn't much care for it, but it stuck. I used to bristle every time I heard someone call me that, but I've gotten used to it over the last few years. The nickname has led to some humorous incidents; for example, a lady would call "Honey," and two of us would show up—her husband and me. I would generally be embarrassed and would cover my embarrassment with the question, "Did you call for me?" The lady would sometimes become embarrassed also and quite often didn't know what to say. Often, the husband would double up with laughter.

Sally had quite a few good laughs over these incidents. I'd been called Honey so much that even my daughter, Ginny, was calling me "Honey." I'd gotten used to it.

Our job on the dude ranch was to keep the dudes busy, if they wanted to stay busy. We did this by taking them out on horseback rides and every week or ten days we'd hold a branding. We staggered our branding throughout the summer so most all of our guests would get a chance to do some real cowboy work, rather than just ride around on scenic horseback rides. Late in the summer the calves would be pretty big and we'd have to team rope them rather than heeling them and dragging them to the fire. The cook would come out and fix up a barbeque for the noon meal and we'd just have cold cuts or something along that line for supper.

Occasionally we'd load a packhorse or two and take some salt out to the cattle on the summer range. After Pat had taken one of these expeditions with some hardy guests, he came to me and said, "Honey, I think you and me need to go check our broodmare bunch. I saw some of what I think were our broodmares, but couldn't locate the stud, having to lead those two packhorses. I think something strange is going on out there."

"When do you want to go?"

"I think we ought to go pretty quick, like tomorrow."

"You think it's that serious?"

"Yep."

The last time Pat had an inkling that something wasn't right with our broodmares, we found a feller, George Crawford, trying to steal some of our colts. We called the sheriff, pressed charges, and George ended up going to prison. I decided we ought to leave in the morning.

"Jimmy can take care of the dude rides with Devin, Blake, an' Quince. We'll leave first thing in the mornin'."

At supper that night, I told the crew what Pat and I had decided for the following day. I lined out Jimmy with what to do and who to send out on what rides.

"You know what horses the dudes are ridin', send Quince out on the short ride an' Devin on the long ride. Don't send more than eight on the long ride an' make sure there ain't any kids under ten on the long ride. Blake can accompany the short ride."

When Sally heard what Pat and I were going to do, she said, "I'm going with you!"

"It might be kinda rough riding," said Pat.

"That's the kind I like," countered Sally.

The following morning, earlier than usual, the horses were run in and Sally, Pat, and I saddled horses. My horses, Roman and Drygulch, were starting to show their age and while they were good for the leisurely dude rides, I wanted to spare them the tougher rides. So I saddled Salty, a horse I'd broke a few years earlier. He had developed into a good horse—he had a good rein, responded well, and it seemed to me that he only had to be taught something once and he knew it.

Sally's horse, Beauty, had injured his shoulder some years earlier. He could handle the slow-paced dude rides, but I thought a rough, long ride might be too much for him. At my suggestion, Sally saddled a younger horse I called Dog. Sally called him Romeo, although I didn't know why. He was a big, rangy-built horse and he could run. I'd broke him a few years earlier and kinda liked him myself.

"This will be a rough day," I told Sally. "Are you sure you want to go?"

"Yes," replied Sally, "I need a break from the ranch and the guests and this will be the perfect excuse. Besides that, I need to know what's going on."

"Suit yourself," I said, "but this won't be a picnic. Speakin' of picnics, I asked the cook to fix us somethin' to eat. Will you an' Pat load the horses in the truck while I go get our grub?"

"Sure, but don't be long."

Just as I was leaving the barn, Walter showed up carrying a big cooler.

"Your noon meal has arrived," he announced, "although it ain't noon yet."

"Good," I said, taking the cooler. "I'll put it in the truck."

"The cook wants to know when you'll be back and if he should leave something out for your supper."

"I don't know when we'll be back," I said, "but it might be a good idea to leave somethin' available for us. It might be a pretty long day."

"Okay, I'll tell him," said Walter.

We loaded the horses, put the cooler in the rear, well behind the horses, and headed out. I wired the cooler to the side of the truck, just in case the road got too rough or there wasn't a road to go on. The sun was just coming up as we left. I always enjoyed watching the sunrise and enjoyed seeing how the colors changed from the dark shades of night into the brilliant colors of the day. However, on this day, I didn't enjoy it so much.

Pat was driving and he seemed to be in a big hurry.

"What's the rush?" I managed to blurt out between the bumps and bouncing around in the cab of the truck.

"I just don't feel good about this," replied Pat.

"Well," I said, "take it easy. We need to get wherever we're goin' alive."

"Honey's right," said Sally. "Whatever damage you suspect has been done is done. We might not be in time to correct it. What do you think is wrong?"

"I dunno," said Pat. "Just got a hunch. But, you're right. There's no need to bust up the truck gettin' there."

I was always surprised at Pat's hunches. I don't know how he got them, but I suspected he would spot something with the binoculars he carried in his saddlebags. On the dude rides he would occasionally stop on a high spot and glass the area around him. I made a mental note to ask him about it later.

Pat slowed down and the ride became more comfortable. We

drove for a couple of hours and didn't see anything amiss. We did notice some of our cows and Sally remarked that, "They are a long way from where they should be."

"They'll head closer to home when the weather starts cooling off," said Pat.

"Don't you think we ought to push them toward the ranch?" It was clear Sally was concerned.

"No," said Pat, "there's plenty of feed and water here. They'll be all right. I'm more concerned about our broodmare bunch."

We drove for another hour or so and occasionally Pat stopped. We all got out of the truck. It was good to stretch our legs, but we didn't stop for that. We were looking for tracks. Horse tracks.

"There's some here," I said, "but they're a couple of days old."

"That's good," said Pat. "We're on the right track."

We got back in the truck and drove farther on. Soon we spotted two mares and colts grazing to our left.

"Here's where the work starts," said Pat.

"Starts," I said. "I feel like I've done a day's work just ridin' out here!"

We found a high spot to unload the horses, tightened the cinches, mounted, and got ready to head out.

"Pat," I said, "this is your deal. You tell us what you want."

"Well, Honey, you and Sally head west for a few miles looking for our horses. I'll head east and make a big circle. Bring any horses you find back here. These mares and colts that are here won't go far. We'll figure out what to do when we meet up. Keep a lookout for the stud. There's definitely something wrong, he wouldn't let these mares go off alone."

We started out on our separate ways. Soon, Sally and I came upon a mare and her colt.

"Remember where she is," I said. "We'll leave her an' look a little farther."

We rode on until we came across two more mares and their colts.

"Darlin', if you want to take these horses back to the truck, I'll go a little farther an' see what I can find. Be sure an' pick up that mare an' her colt we saw earlier. I want to see if I can find the stud. Somethin's happened to him. Just wait at the truck until Pat or I show up. I can't figure these mares bein' scattered like they are. You can get somethin' to eat from the cooler. If you spot any more horses, pick 'em up"

I headed off, confident Sally could take the horses back to the truck. It wasn't long before I found another mare and her colt. I thought it best to take this pair to Sally, then I could continue searching.

I found Sally and left the mare and colt in her care. I told her, "I want to look over that ridge. If there's nothin' there, I want to look over the next one. I'll meet you back at the truck."

I headed out again. I figured we had six mares and their colts. I tried to remember how many mares we had in that broodmare bunch, twenty-five or -six I thought.

When I got to the top of the ridge, I saw Sally slowly making her way toward the truck. Off to the east I saw some dust and thought Pat had found some horses. From the dust that was being raised, I figured he'd found more horses than Sally and I had.

I started down the ridge, not seeing anything in the valley. I decided to climb the next ridge and if I didn't find anything, I'd head back toward Sally and help her or perhaps head toward Pat and see if I could give him a hand.

When I topped the second ridge and looked into the valley, I could see some horses at the far end. I couldn't tell how many, maybe five or six. I stopped at the top of the ridge to give Salty a breather and tried to figure out the easiest way to herd the horses toward where I could meet Sally or the truck.

Having devised a plan, I headed out. I swung around farther to the west, figuring on moving the horses east and meeting up somewhere with Sally. The horses saw me and started running east. I thought, *Those horses are actin' more like wild horses than our broodmare bunch!*

I kept the horses heading east, hoping when they met Sally's bunch that they'd slow down. I didn't push them, I didn't want a horse race going on, but I stayed close enough to keep them in sight.

When they topped the ridge, I lost sight of them and increased my speed. I slowed down as I topped the ridge and spotted the horses ahead of me. They had slowed down to a leisurely trot and didn't seem alarmed.

The horses continued down the valley for a way then started up another ridge. I thought if they crossed this ridge, they would meet up with Sally.

Once again, they disappeared from sight as they crossed the ridge. I hurried up the ridge so I could keep the horses in sight.

I got to the top of the ridge and stopped to let Salty get his wind. I saw Sally's little bunch of horses, but couldn't see Sally. The horses I'd been following joined Sally's bunch and slowed down to a walk. I finally saw Sally off to the east bringing a mare and colt to the bunch.

I trotted down to Sally.

"Looks like you've brought me some more horses," she said. "How many?"

"I dunno." I said, "I never got a count on 'em."

"I didn't get a good look at them, but I don't think they're all ours," said Sally.

"We'll take 'em all anyway," I said.

"I think there's a donkey with them," said Sally.

"Really?" I couldn't believe I'd brought in a donkey. We were looking for horses. I had noticed a smaller critter following the bunch, but figured it was a colt—it was spotted. "If there's a donkey there, he's got to be wild. Let's not push 'em too hard, he might booger our deal."

"Right," said Sally.

"I saw some dust off to the east when I was up on the ridge. I think I'll head over that way an' see if Pat needs a hand. Just keep these horses headin' toward the truck."

"And the donkey!"

"Yeah," I said. I could see Sally was trying to give me a hard time. I hadn't figured on capturing a donkey.

I headed toward the east where I had seen the dust earlier. I swung farther south thinking I didn't want to run into Pat bringing more horses. I got to the top of a ridge and rested Salty as I looked for any sign of Pat. I finally spotted some dust about two miles back to the northeast and headed that direction.

When I reached Pat, he was having a hard time keeping the horses headed west. I saw his problem and swung around where I could help him. We finally got the horses headed in a northwest direction, but didn't have a chance to visit. It was a full-time job keeping the horses headed where we wanted them to go.

I could tell Pat's horse was about played out so I took the east side of the herd where the horses wanted to go. The two of us finally managed to keep the herd under control and eased them toward where we would either meet Sally or find the truck.

We finally got to the truck where we found Sally slowly circling her horse herd, which was grazing. The horses Pat and I brought joined Sally's horses and started to graze. All three of us continued to circle the horse herd until they all settled down. Then we went to the truck to get something to eat.

We loosened the cinches on our saddles, hobbled our horses, and started to eat. As we ate, we talked about what had happened during the day.

Sally told how we had split up and I'd brought in another mare and colt, then ran in six pairs and a donkey.

"I saw the donkey," said Pat. "How come you brought him?"

"I didn't have a choice," I replied. "You brought in fifteen or twenty. Where'd you find 'em?"

"I found a couple of little bunches and put them together, then found two pairs and that young mustang stud. That stud gave me some real problems. He kept drivin' the mares back on me. If you hadn't showed up when you did, I'd have lost the whole bunch. My horse was about done."

"You mean he did something good besides bringing in a donkey?" I could see Sally was going to harass me constantly about the donkey.

"Yep," replied Pat, "and I'm glad. How many we got?"

"Counting the donkey?"

"Nope."

"I think we've got seventeen of our mares and I think they all have colts," said Sally. "Then there's the young stud, three mustang mares, their colts, and the donkey. That's twenty-two, not counting the colts."

"The young stud is going to give us some problems," said Pat. "If I had a gun, I'd fix him permanently."

I knew what Pat was thinking and thought that the young stud had really given Pat a tough time.

"Well, we ain't got a gun, but we can fix him," I said. "I can rope his head, Sally can catch his hind feet, and Pat, you can fix him permanently. Then we'll hobble him, left front to right rear, an' take him home with us. It'll slow us down some, but we'll make it. We can hobble the mustang mares if they give us a problem."

"Sounds like a plan," said Pat.

"How many mares were in that stud bunch?"

"If I remember right," said Sally, "there were twenty-six."

"That means we're still missin' nine of our mares," I said. "Plus the stud. Soon as we finish eatin' we'll fix the stud, then start toward the ranch. We probably ought to keep goin' all night if necessary."

"That won't be necessary," said Pat. "We can corral the horses in that old set of corrals on the south end of the ranch, then come and get them tomorrow with the truck. We'll be late gettin' home tonight as it is. It will mean two or three trips, but we can bring some hay for the horses we have to leave in the corrals."

"That'll work," I said. "Let's go fix the young stud an' get movin'."

We got our horses, tightened the cinches, and went to catch the mustang stud. "Make sure your cinch is tight," I told Sally. "Why you tightenin' your cinch, Pat?"

"Just in case you miss," replied Pat. "That stud is a wild horse and we'll probably only get one shot at him."

Remembering what Pat had said about a gun and his comment about only having one shot at him, I resolved to make my first loop count.

I rode toward the young stud, he was grazing beside a mare. My rope was ready. When he raised his head to see what was happening,

I threw my rope without swinging it. The loop was true and I hastily took my dallies before the loop settled low on the stud's neck.

The stud fought the rope, but Salty held him.

"Get his hind feet, Sally!"

Sally's first loop missed and that surprised me because Sally was such a good roper. But her second loop was true and we had the young stud stretched out.

"You get to do the honors, Pat," I said.

"It will be a pleasure," replied Pat, taking out his knife.

"Make sure you tie off the cords good," I said.

Pat cut the end of the scrotum exposing the stones. He tied off the cords using hair pulled from the young stud's tail.

"It'll be a few days, but I bet your attitude will improve," said Pat. "Keep him down and I'll see if we have some blood stopper in the truck and a piece of rope to hobble him with."

Pat went to the truck and Sally and I kept the young, now gelding, stretched out. While we were waiting for Pat to return, I said to Sally, "How come you missed your first loop? I thought you were a better roper than that."

"You didn't move the horse forward, like I'd planned," she said. "By the way, what do you call that throw you made to catch the horse?"

Pat had returned with a piece of soft cotton rope he'd found behind the seat of the truck and a bottle of medicine. "This blood stopper is out-dated, but it's all we got. Yes, what do you call that throw?"

Pat applied the blood stopper then started to fashion cross hobbles on the young horse.

"I don't have a name for that throw, I'm still perfecting it," I said. "Better go with the right front to the left rear seein' as he's lyin' on his left side. You'll stand a lesser chance of gettin' kicked. When he calls for some slack, give it to him, Sally."

Pat hobbled the horse, took my rope off his neck and took off Sally's heel rope. Not knowing he was free, the horse just laid there. Pat gave him a little kick and the horse struggled to his feet. He tried to run off, but couldn't, and fell down. He was hobbled.

"It'll take him a while to get used to the hobbles," said Pat. "But he'll figure it out if he's got any sense."

"Pat," I said, "you load your horse an' take the truck an' go ahead of the horses. You know where the corrals are an' your horse has had enough for today. If you can find a road, take it. Sally, you lead the horses and follow Pat. Keep 'em at a slow trot, some of the colts have had a pretty rough day. I'll bring up the rear."

Sally asked, "You won't let your donkey get away, will you?"

"Certainly not! That donkey has become very valuable!"

"Valuable! How come?"

"Because," I replied, "as you said, he belongs to me!"

Pat loaded his horse, unsaddled him, and cinched his saddle to the side rack of the truck. He started out and Sally followed. I had a little tough time getting the horses started, but they soon followed Sally. The young ex-stud followed, showing signs of his recent operation and having a little trouble adjusting to his hobbles.

We crossed a small creek and Pat stopped on the other side. Sally stopped and all the horses had a chance to drink. Pat unloaded his horse on a high spot and let him drink.

I watered Salty and rode over to where Pat was loading his horse.

"It's a good thing you stopped," I said to Pat. "I'd plum forgot about waterin' these horses, an' they'll be in a corral overnight."

"Are they gettin' some grazing along the way? They'll be off feed overnight," said Pat.

"They're gettin' some as we go along," I replied.

"It'll be dark by the time we reach the corrals," said Pat. "Let 'em eat as much as they can."

Camping Out

We let the horses drink as much as they wanted then started out again. Pat found a road and the going was a little easier. I had a little problem keeping the mustang mares with the rest of the bunch, but managed.

The sun was going down when we reached the old corrals. Pat had walked around the corrals and met me at the gate.

"These corrals should hold 'em tonight, if they don't press on 'em too hard," he said, as he closed the gate behind Sally.

"I'll back up to the chute, we can load your horses and head for home. We'll be late gettin' there as it is."

"Sounds good to me," I said.

"Me too," added Sally.

On the way back to the ranch we discussed the activities for the next few days. We'd certainly need to pick up the horses at the corrals, which might take three or four trips, two days at best. We'd need to decide what to do with the mustang mares and their colts, the new gelding, and my new donkey. We were still out nine mares and the stud and we'd have to find them. Although I didn't say anything, I suspected we'd need to buy another stallion if we wanted to stay in the paint horse business. A stallion just doesn't leave his mares to wander the country.

I began to think that I should get a couple of saddle horses, a packhorse, a tent and bedroll, some groceries, and come back, prepared to stay until I found our horses. Nine mares and their colts represented a sizeable loss if they were not found.

I thought it best to go alone. Pat was needed to handle the dudes and Sally needed to oversee the whole ranch operation. In my mind, I was the logical choice as everyone else had duties to be done on a daily basis.

We reached the ranch house well after dark. We took care of our horses and grained them well. The cook had left some supper for us, but it needed to be heated. Sally started to heat it for us when Bud came into the kitchen.

"You still up? I thought you'd be in bed a long time ago," I said.

"I've been waiting for you, curious to know what's going on," said Bud.

"You shouldn't have waited up, Daddy. You know we'd fill you in come morning."

"Pat told me earlier what he thought was going on and I wanted to see if he was right."

"You know he's almost always right," said Sally.

"Yes, but tell me what is happening," replied Bud.

Sally told Bud about the day's activities, not failing to mention that I had brought in a donkey.

"A donkey, huh? You seem to have an affinity for them," said Bud. "As I recall, you first showed up here with a donkey."

"That's correct," I said, "and I brought her back the second year at your request." I wasn't going to let everyone harass me about the donkey.

At my comment, Bud was willing to let the donkey matter drop. But he did ask, "What's the plan?"

I outlined my tentative plan about taking a few days to look for the mares and camp for a few days. I could leave after we brought the captured horses home.

"That sounds good to me," said Bud.

As an afterthought, I said, "We might want to start lookin' for another stallion if we want to stay in the paint horse business. None of us saw anythin' of the stud an' a stud just doesn't leave his mares. That young stud that we gelded had some of our mares."

"Yes," said Bud, "it doesn't look good. That stud was starting to get some age on him. How old was he, Sally?"

"I think he was pushing seventeen or eighteen," replied Sally.

"More like nineteen or twenty," said Pat.

"No matter," said Bud. "We'd best start looking. The old stud had served us well."

"We've got that other stud up on the north range," said Sally. "We can put a few more mares with him."

"There's not a big rush to get another stallion," said Bud. "We can give that younger stud thirty or so mares and take our time looking for another stud. But we'll keep our eyes open for another one. When are you planning on going camping, Honey?"

"As soon as we bring the strayed horses back," I said.

I spent the next day hauling horses from the old corrals to the ranch. I'd put some hay in the truck to feed the horses we couldn't haul. I would have liked to get them some water, but couldn't do it. They'd just have to tough it out. Sally and Ginny came with me the first day, but didn't the second—the ride was too much for Ginny.

I managed to get all the horses back to the ranch in two days. I was real late getting back to the ranch the second day because I had to make three trips. I'd considered leaving the few horses in the corral another day, but I thought three days without water was too much. I'd left instructions to keep all the horses in a corral until I got all them hauled in. This would allow the colts to mother up with the mares if I couldn't bring home pairs.

That night, even though it was late, I made preparations to leave the next morning to hunt the missing horses. I was surprised to see Sally packing her stuff.

"What are you doin'?"

"I'm going with you," answered Sally.

"I don't think that's a good idea," I said.

"Why not?"

"This will be a pretty rough trip," I said.

"That's all right," said Sally. "I can handle it. Besides, you'll need a camp cook. And when I'm not cooking, I can look for horses. Two of us can cover more ground than one."

"Who's goin' to watch the ranch?"

"Daddy's here, Pat's here, and Jimmy and Chuck. They should

be able to handle it. Besides, I don't feel like I did enough the other day."

"You did plenty," I said. "You brought in those horses I pushed on you an' you even brought in my donkey!"

Sally laughed. "That's right, but I still didn't do enough. You and Pat did all the rough work."

"I guess if you're insistent, you can go. Better tell the cook to get enough groceries for two for at least four days."

"I already have," said Sally.

"I was thinkin' of takin' a packhorse, but I think we'll take the two-ton truck and forget about packin'. We'll need the extra room for your stuff," I said, grinning.

"Very funny, Cowboy," replied Sally, as she gave me a kiss. "This will almost be like a second honeymoon!"

"Oh," I said, trying to sound disappointed and disgruntled.

"You didn't like the first one?"

I had to be careful here. I was trying to have a little fun, but at this point it could turn out to be less than expected. Trying to sound businesslike, I said, "Certainly I liked the first one. Why do you think I've kept you around so long? But on the first one, we didn't have nine valuable horses to find. You need to remember this is business work!"

"I'm well aware of that, Honey," said Sally, with a mischievous grin on her face. "And you squirmed out of that one nicely. But I thought you kept me around because I can rope pretty well."

"I saw you miss the heels on that mustang we cut. That didn't impress me."

"Everyone's entitled to one miss each day," replied Sally, "and I've seen you use up a whole week's worth at one branding!"

I couldn't reply to that, she was a good roper, better than me, and it surprised me that she had missed the heels on that mustang. Sally had me wrapped around her little finger and she knew it. Surprisingly, I knew it too, but it didn't bother me much. We continued to pack, doing some good-natured bantering back and forth.

The next morning we loaded the horses. I took Salty and two other colts I'd named Squirt and Mistake. Sally took Cupid and

15

Sweet Pea along with Romeo, the one I called Dog. We also threw some extra halters and hobbles in the truck, nine to be exact.

Before we headed out Pat came to me. He handed me a .22 caliber pistol. "This won't do much, except at short range, but you might need it. If you go about two miles farther south from where we unloaded our horses the other day, you'll find an old riverbed. I don't know if there's any water in it. If there isn't water, you go a couple of miles farther, there's a windmill that waters the cattle for the neighbors. It will make a good camp. There's also corrals there. It'll be easier if you stay on the road. It'll take you right to the windmill. It's pretty well worn out, but it'll be better than bouncing through the sagebrush."

He handed me a box of shells for the pistol. "I hope you don't need these," he said.

I knew what he meant. "I hope not either," I said. I put the pistol behind the seat of the truck while Sally, Jimmy, and Devin loaded our supplies.

"If you're not back in three days, I'll bring your truck and come lookin' for you," said Pat.

"If you come lookin' for us, better bring some more groceries. If we haven't found our horses by then, we'll just have to keep lookin'," I said.

We headed out on what I suspected Sally thought would be a fun camping trip. It was a better ride on the old worn-out road than making our own road through the sagebrush, like we had done when Sally, Pat, and myself headed out previously.

When I figured we should be reaching the old riverbed, Sally spotted some horses off in the distance.

"This is where the work begins and the sight seein' trip ends," I said. "I'll unload a horse, saddle him, and check out those horses. You keep goin' till you reach the windmill. Unload our horses, hobble 'em an' turn 'em loose. If those horses you saw are ours, I'll bring 'em in an' we can keep 'em in the corral overnight. You can set up camp an' start supper if you want."

"Yes sir, Honey," said Sally.

As I saddled my horse I began to wonder if I was becoming too much of a boss. I'd given Sally orders just like she was one of the hands, not the half owner of the ranch and my wife. I decided I'd talk with her about it. I pulled the cinch tight and climbed aboard Mistake.

I leaned out of the saddle to kiss Sally goodbye and said, "I'll see you at camp."

That's where I made my mistake. I'd forgotten to untrack Mistake and when I started him out at what I thought would be a fast trot, he bogged his head and started to buck! I heard Sally laughing and heard her holler, "Ride him, Cowboy!"

I had to ride him. He was the only horse I had saddled. After a few jumps, I got his head pulled up and got him lined out toward the horses Sally had pointed out to me. He wanted to run and I had a hard time holding him back.

"Better slow down an' save your strength for later," I told the horse. "You might need it!"

I saw the horses and noticed one spotted horse in the bunch. I wasn't sure where the windmill was, but started the horses in the direction I thought it was. I could see the dust from the truck as Sally headed down the old road. The horses didn't start running, just trotted off in the direction I pointed them.

These must be broke horses, not wild horses, I thought as I followed the horses. *With a little luck they'll take me straight to the windmill.*

I continued to follow the horses and soon saw the windmill and the corrals. The truck was there, but Sally was nowhere in sight. The horses weren't unloaded, but the truck was backed up to the loading chute. I noticed one of the horses was gone and Sally's saddle was missin from the side of the truck.

I corralled the horses and let Mistake get a drink. *Fine time to go off pleasure ridin',* I thought. *Guess I'll have to set up camp.* I put Mistake in a separate pen and started to unload the horses when I saw a herd of horses headed toward the corral. I put the horses I'd corralled in a separate pen and opened the gate into the big corral.

Sally had spotted another bunch of horses so when she reached the corrals, she saddled Sweet Pea and went out to investigate. She was bringing these horses to the corral. Sally followed the horses into the corral and I closed the gate behind her.

"I thought you'd have camp set up an' supper ready," I said.

"Well, I saw these horses, noticed two paints and thought I'd better have a closer look at them. The two paints are ours. What did you get?"

"I saw one paint with those horses you spotted," I said, "but haven't got close enough to see if she's ours. My horses are in that pen over there."

"Looks like you brought four, five, no six horses," said Sally as we walked toward the pen. "And that one paint is ours. That bay mare might be ours, but I need to get a closer look. There were some solid-colored horses in that stud bunch."

Sally looked over the bay mare, but I spotted our brand on her before Sally.

"She's ours all right. An' those two spotted colts are ours, too. Do those two paint mares you brought have colts?"

"Yes. Aren't you glad you brought me along? We've got almost half our missing horses already."

"I guess so. But it's gettin' late. We better set up camp. I'll unload our horses, hobble 'em, give 'em some grain an' turn 'em loose. If you want to start supper, I'll pitch the tent. We'll keep these horses we found in overnight an' sort 'em in the mornin'."

"It sounds like a plan to me," said Sally. "What do you want for supper, peanut butter and jelly sandwiches?"

"I'd really rather have steak." I was hoping Sally was kidding about peanut butter sandwiches. I found out later she was.

By the time I threw the horses some hay and pitched the tent, Sally had supper ready. It was steak and it was good!

As we ate, we talked. We decided we'd had a fairly successful day. We'd found four of our nine missing horses. We only had five more to find. At one point, I asked Sally, "Do you think I'm becomin' too bossy? I got to thinkin' about it when I rode off an' I was guilty of givin' you orders just like you were one of the hired hands. How do you feel about that?"

"I'm comfortable with it," said Sally. "In fact, I'm a little proud of you taking over like you have. Someone has to be boss and take responsibility for this outfit. You've done a good job and even Daddy says you've done better than he expected."

"You mean he expected less of me?"

"No, silly. He expected a lot from you. You have delivered more."

"I'm glad to hear that," I said. "Sometimes I wonder if I'm pullin' my share of the load."

"Don't worry about that, Honey."

"But look at you," I said. "You're as good a hand as we've ever had, not only with the cattle but with the horses, too! An' you do the hirin', train the maids, do the payroll, pay the bills, take care of Ginny, look out after the needs of the dudes, an' you've fixed a terrific supper tonight, in addition to findin' just as many of our horses as I did. Compared to all that, I feel like I'm only doin' part of the job."

"If you really feel that way, you can come and help the maids anytime you want! But let's look at what you do. You train the new wranglers, halter break the weaner colts in the winter, pull the bullers for breeding in the replacement heifer program, break the two-year-old colts, and generally oversee the dudes in addition to managing the cow herd and scheduling the brandings. You've got plenty to do."

"It doesn't seem like it," I said.

"That's because you're a cowboy and it's all just part of the job to you. So you do it."

I didn't have an answer, so I said, "Let's turn in, it's been a big day an' there's no tellin' what tomorrow will bring."

"That's a good idea," said Sally. "But not before we do the dishes. I'll wash and you dry."

While we were doing the dishes, Sally thought she would have a little fun with me. She asked, "What set off Mistake earlier today?"

"I was in a rush," I said, "an' I forgot to untrack him. An' I forgot there was a little buck in him."

"That sounds like something a dude would do," said Sally.

"Maybe bein' around the dudes is rubbin' off on me," I said. "I have been around 'em a lot lately."

"No," said Sally. "You'll have to come up with something better than that!"

"Well," I said, "I didn't want to lose 'em, so I tried to hurry."

"Mistake had you loosened up in the saddle. Another jump or two and you might have lost him."

"I was aware of that. It's a good thing I stopped him when I did."

"You stopped him?"

"Yes," I said. "I finally got his head pulled up."

Sally laughed. "That's a good story."

I could see I was losing in this good-natured bickering. "Here," I said as I handed a tin plate back to Sally, "this plate ain't clean, wash it again."

Disaster

The next morning, Sally was up before the sun and had a fire going. Coffee was hot when she brought a cup to me in the tent.

"Breakfast in bed, huh?"

"Yes sir," replied Sally. "Only the best for the best."

"Well," I said, "it's about time I got the respect I truly deserve! How come I'm not treated like this every day?"

"Because we don't get a chance to go camping every day," said Sally.

"I guess you know I'll be lookin' forward to this in the future," I said. "Maybe I'll set up a tent in the bedroom. Do you think that would help?"

"I know it wouldn't, silly. What's the plan for today?"

"I guess we'll start lookin' for horses. What's for breakfast?"

"Bacon and eggs," replied Sally. "I better check on them."

Sally left the tent and I got out of bed and got dressed. Sally was just fixing a plate when I left the tent.

"I was going to bring this to you so you could have a real breakfast in bed," she said, as she handed me a plate.

"That would have been nice," I said, "but we have too much to do today. We need to get started, the sun's already up."

"Where are we going first?"

"Just pick a direction."

"We ought to go west."

"Why?"

"I really don't want to ride east and have to look into the sun all morning," replied Sally.

"West it is," I said.

We each had another cup of coffee before saddling our horses. I threw the horses some hay and saddled Squirt and Sally saddled Cupid.

Remembering yesterday and the adventure I had with Mistake, I reminded myself and Sally, "Don't forget to untrack your horse!"

Sally laughed and said, "Don't *you* forget!"

After we untracked our horses and mounted, we rode off. Thinking I'd have a little fun, I started off to the east, but Sally hollered, "That's the wrong direction, Cowboy! This way is west!"

I turned around, grinning, and we headed off to the west.

"It's a good thing you brought me along," said Sally. "You'd have got lost before we even left camp!"

"Maybe you're right," I said.

As we rode, we talked. "If we find a few more horses, we'll need more hay," I said. "There wasn't room enough to bring more hay in the truck."

We rode for a couple of hours without finding any horses. I'd been checking the ground as we rode and hadn't seen any fresh signs of horses. We'd gotten about twelve miles away from camp and decided to turn south and make a big circle back to camp.

"We could cover more ground if we split up," said Sally.

"Probably," I said. "You gettin' tired of my company already?" I didn't want to say it, but I thought it best we stay together. This was new country to both Sally and me, and I didn't want to risk Sally getting lost.

"No, Honey. I was just thinking of finding horses," replied Sally.

"Well," I said, "you could ride up that ridge, look on the other side an' I'll ride up this ridge. We need to keep in sight of each other. If you see some horses, signal an' I'll do the same."

We split up and rode separately for about an hour. Occasionally I'd lose sight of Sally, but she'd come back into sight again. When I couldn't see her, she'd ridden down the other side of the ridge to check out a draw.

At one point, she came to the top of the ridge and began waving her arms, her hat in one hand. I saw her and knew she'd found something. I put Squirt into a fast trot and soon met Sally on the other ridge. I was surprised when I met her, her face was tear-stained and smeared where she had wiped her tears and dust away from her face. She had been crying!

"What's the matter? Are you all right?"

"I found one of our pairs," replied Sally, wiping away more tears. "The mare is dead and her colt is staying around close. It's Star Fire, one of my favorite horses. I rode her quite a bit when I was growing up."

"Let's go look," I said. "You lead the way."

Sally led the way to the dead mare. Her colt was close by, not knowing what was happening, but showing obvious signs of distress.

I surveyed the situation. The ground was torn up all around the mare and the grass had been uprooted. It looked like there had been a struggle, but there were no signs of a predator. There was no blood on the ground, although the signs pointed toward a violent death.

Sally asked, "What could have caused this?"

"I'm not sure," I said. I was searching my memory for a possible answer. "It might have been brain fever …"

"Encephalitis," interrupted Sally. "I know something about it—it's carried by mosquitoes."

"There's nothing we can do for her now," I said. "I'll rope the colt an' we'll take him back to camp."

I took down my rope, made a loop and tried to catch the colt. My first loop missed, but Sally had made a loop and caught the colt on her first try. I marveled at Sally's roping—she was good!

I got off my horse, hobbled him, and told Sally, "Trip him up an' put him on the ground. I'll fashion a halter that won't choke him an' we'll take him to camp."

Sally did as she was told, although I'm sure it hurt her to trip the colt. As soon as he was on the ground, I got on his head, held him down, and made a halter that wouldn't choke him.

Before I let the colt up, I told Sally, "He'll probably fight this some, just let him. If he heads toward camp, let him. It'll take us the rest of the day to get back to camp, and he should be halter broke by then. I'll follow along behind an' encourage him when he needs it."

Sally let the colt fight the halter while I unhobbled my horse and got on. The way back to camp was slow and the colt threw himself a few times. A slap on the rump or side with my lariat would get the colt up and we'd proceed. Occasionally the colt would balk but a tightening on Sally's rope and a slap on the rump from my rope would get him moving again. Soon he was following Sally's horse without any encouragement from me.

The sun was almost set when we reached camp. The colt was broke to lead and Sally made the comment, "I've got this colt broke to lead already. That's one less colt you have to halter break this winter. You know, the more you have me around, the easier I make your job!"

I couldn't argue with that, she was a good hand!

"I'll take care of the horses if you want to start supper," I said.

"I can take care of my horse," replied Sally.

We got to the corral and Sally led the orphaned colt inside. I closed the gate and slowly worked my way up Sally's rope to free the colt from the homemade halter. While the colt had learned how to lead and learned some respect for the rope, he hadn't learned respect for humans. I couldn't get close to the colt without him fighting. Finally, Sally snubbed him up close and I took off the crude halter, but not before patting him between the ears and apologizing for how roughly he had been treated during the trip back to camp. When the colt was free, he immediately jumped away and joined the other horses.

We grained and unsaddled our horses and turned them loose in the corral. Sally went to fix supper and I threw hay to the horses.

As we ate supper, steak again, we discussed the day's activities. We had only found one horse and she was dead, but we had her colt.

"What's the plan for tomorrow?"

"Well," I answered, "we have found half our missin' horses. We still have three mares an' colts plus the stud to find. But, we're run-nin' short of hay. I think, if it's all right with you, I'll send a load of horses back to the ranch with you. You can bring more hay when you come back. You can have Devin, Blake, Chuck, an' Quince load the hay for you."

"And what will you be doing while I'm gone?"

"Since you don't like to ride into the sun, I'll ride to the east an' see what I can find."

"Do you want to take the wild mares and colts in also?"

"Yep. We can run 'em through the sale when we have time to go to town. It'll be some extra money."

The next morning while Sally was fixing breakfast, I sorted our saddle horses from the rest and parked the truck at the loading chute. When I was sure Sally wasn't looking, I took the pistol Pat had given me and hid it in the brush by the loading chute. I wasn't sure I would need it, but if the stud had become a victim of brain fever, I needed to be prepared.

After breakfast we loaded the mares and colts in the truck. As Sally prepared to leave, she said, "Don't forget to do the dishes this morning!"

"And don't you get lost," I replied.

As I did the morning dishes, I watched the dust disappear as Sally left for the ranch. Dishes done, I saddled Salty and rode to the east. I rode for a few hours, but felt encouraged. I was seeing more fresh signs of horses, but hadn't seen any horses. I rode farther and started to circle around to the south figuring I'd go back to camp in the general direction Sally and I had taken the orphaned colt yesterday.

I topped a ridge and spotted some horses in the draw below me. I couldn't tell, but it looked like there was a donkey or two with the horses. I paused before I started toward the horses. If those donkeys were wild, I needed to start them in the right direction if I was go-ing to try and corral them. I'd left the gate to the main corral open, as our saddle horses were in a separate corral.

When I figured out what to do, I started the horses. They were headed the right direction, I just needed to keep them moving that way, careful not to get them running. They were going at a trot and I thought if I could keep them going at that speed, I shouldn't have a problem corralling them. The horses were leading and the donkeys followed, although one of the donkeys acted like a stud horse, following behind and trying to herd the mares. There were two spotted mares in the bunch and I was sure they were ours, and they had spotted colts by their sides.

We followed the draw and curved around in a dry creekbed. We topped a little hill and I was surprised to see a set of corrals at the bottom of the draw and the horses were headed right toward the corrals. There was a windmill at the corrals and I was thinking we were closer to camp than I had thought.

The horses headed right into the corrals, but the one donkey turned away. Apparently the horses had been using the corrals to water at, but the donkey refused to enter. I rushed to the corrals and closed the gate. It didn't matter to me that I hadn't caught the one donkey, I had the horses! That was easier than I had anticipated. I looked over the horses I had caught. Two of the mares were ours, the other mare didn't have a brand on her and neither did the donkey. Now I had only one mare to find along with the stud.

I hobbled my horse and walked around the corral. I had to tie up a pole in one spot and wire it with some baling wire I found. But something was wrong! Our saddle horses weren't in sight and neither was the tent!

I had to laugh at myself. I thought I had made it back to my camp, but found another set of corrals instead! Contented that the corrals would hold the horses and one donkey, I started to follow the old road that led away from the corrals. I followed the old road for a few miles when I came upon a cow camp nestled in some cottonwood trees. There was a set of corrals close by and a couple of hobbled horses. One was saddled. There was an old pickup truck parked in front of the cabin.

I rode toward the cabin and hollered, "Hello the house!"

Presently a man appeared at the door. He walked with a limp and hadn't shaved for a time.

"Howdy," he said.

"Hello," I replied.

He asked, "What brings you out this way?"

"I'm from the Wilson Ranch. I'm lookin' for some stray horses from our stud bunch. I found some an' got 'em corralled in an old set of corrals back up the road a piece. Also got a broomtail mare an' her colt an' a donkey with 'em."

"Bud Wilson's? You find the stud?"

"Yep an' nope. I'm Bud's son-in-law."

"You the one they call Honey?"

"Yep," I replied, bristling somewhat that my nickname should be known so far away from home.

"I've heard about you. Paint stud?"

"Yep."

"Your stud is over that hill," he said, pointing off to the west. "No need to go looking for him, he's dead."

"Dead?"

"Yep. I shot him."

"You shot him? What for?"

"Put him out of his misery. He was thrashin' around, actin' like he was in pain or he'd lost his senses. I put an end to it real quick."

Brain fever, I thought.

"Might as well get down and get something to eat. I'm just fixing dinner now."

I hadn't noticed, but it was well past noon. I got off my horse, hobbled him, and turned him loose.

As I entered the cabin, the old cowpuncher said, "How is old Bud anyhow?"

"He's okay," I answered, "considerin'."

"I'd heard he was confined to a wheelchair. How does he like that?"

"He don't," I replied. "But it just slows him down a little."

"Well, you tell him I said hello when you see him."

"I can do that," I said, "but who are you?"

"Don't you know me? I thought everyone had heard of me. I'm Dusty Waters!"

"Dusty Waters? Why that's mud!"

"Yep, that's what they call me, Mud. Here, eat this."

We sat down to eat and I tried to think if Bud had ever mentioned Dusty Waters or Mud. I couldn't recall him ever saying anything.

"I thought I might find an easy way to get a truck to the corrals where I've got our mares by followin' this road. I'm camped about ten miles from where the corrals are, at another set of corrals."

"You're camped at Cedar Springs," said Mud. "The corrals where you've got these other horses is Dry Springs. You can drive a truck from one to the other, but it's a pretty rough road. You'll go right past here again. It'll take you a couple of hours. You're probably twenty miles away from Cedar Springs by the road, but only ten or so by cuttin' cross-country."

We finished eating and I asked Mud for more detailed instructions on how to get to Dry Springs by road.

"Don't need more instructions," said Mud, "there's only the one road."

I thanked Mud for dinner, caught up Salty, took off the hobbles and rode off. I went cross-country, figuring on saving a few hours. By the time I got back to camp, it was almost dark.

I was surprised to find a spotted mare and her colt outside the corral. I opened the gate and put her and the colt inside. I unsaddled Salty, grained him, threw some hay to the horses, and started supper. I didn't need much to eat, Mud had fed me pretty well. I was surprised that Sally hadn't shown up.

After I ate, I cleaned the dishes and got ready for bed. I was becoming concerned for Sally, she should have been here by now. What if she'd had truck problems or something? I fell asleep thinking I'd give Sally until noon the next day to show up, then I'd go looking for her.

The next morning I fixed coffee then went to look over the mare and colt I'd captured the night before. I was sure they were ours, they were used to people being around. They hadn't run off when I corralled them.

Satisfied that I had accounted for all our horses, even though the stud was dead, I had another cup of coffee and thought about going out to look for Sally. I was afraid that she had had truck problems.

It wasn't long before I saw dust rising from the old road. *That must be Sally,* I thought.

Before long, Sally came bouncing down the road with about half a load of hay.

"Miss me, Honey?"

"Yes," I replied. "I was afraid you'd broke down or had some trouble. I expected you last night."

"No. It was late when I got to the ranch so I decided to stay over. I did get a nice hot bath. What did you do?"

"I've got all our missing horses, or at least got them accounted for," I said.

"Accounted for? What do you mean?"

"Well, our stud is dead. But I've got all our missin' mares plus a broomtail an' her colt an' a donkey."

"Another donkey?"

"Yep. You've got too much hay. We don't need it now. Our job's done here. What's happenin' back at the ranch?"

"Nothing new," replied Sally. "They seem to be getting along perfectly well without us. What are we going to do with this hay?"

"I know a place where we can put it," I said. "Let's get busy."

We unloaded part of the hay, enough to feed the horses that night, and with the rest of the hay, we got in the truck and started toward Dusty Water's cow camp. It took us a couple of hours to get to Mud's camp and I told Sally about what I'd done the day before.

Mud wasn't at his camp, but we unloaded the hay in what appeared to be a stackyard. We were almost done when Mud came riding up.

"I really don't need any feed now," said Mud, as he slowly climbed off his horse.

I could tell by the way he got off his horse that his riding days were about over. He'd seen better days in the past.

"But you will come fall," I said. "Do you want that broomtail an' colt I've got corralled at Dry Springs? An' what about the donkey?"

29

"I guess so, although I don't know what I'll do with 'em."

"They're yours," I said. "By the way, this is my wife, Bud's daughter, Sally."

"Pleased to see you again, ma'am," said Mud, taking off his hat.

"Again? You'll have to forgive me, I don't remember ever meeting you," said Sally.

"I don't figure you do," said Mud. "Last time I saw you, you were still in diapers."

"We'll take the truck an' get your broomtails an' donkey, bring 'em to you then go back an' get our horses."

"I'd appreciate that," said Mud. "I ain't got good transportation for hauling a broomtail. Here, I got something for you."

Mud reached into his saddlebag and brought out a piece of hide. It had the Wilson brand on it.

"I went up this morning and cut this brand off the stud horse I shot, just so you'd know the horse was dead. By the way, there's an unbranded bull runnin' around here. A maverick. If any of your cows get down this far you could end up havin' your calving season year round. I've tried to corral him, but he's pretty wild, been that way for a long time."

I asked, "Might you be wantin' some help gettin' him captured?" It sounded to me like Mud was asking for some help, in a roundabout way.

"Sometimes I feel like I could use some," replied Mud. "I can't hardly get close to him. I've been fairly close to him, but he's turned on me and my horse and put us on the run. He sure is wild."

I took the piece of hide and put it under the seat of the truck. Sally and I headed toward Dry Springs with an empty truck. When we got to the corrals, we separated the broomtail and her colt and the donkey from our horses and loaded them in the truck and took them to Mud's. When we got to Mud's, he insisted we eat the noon meal with him, but we declined. I thought it would be well after dark if we stayed and ate with him.

We headed back to Dry Springs, loaded our mares and colts and started back to our camp. We drove right by Mud's camp, it didn't look like anyone was home.

On the way back, Sally and I talked about Mud's situation. Sally made the comment, "Perhaps we should come back and try to corral that wild bull."

"I don't know that we have time for that," I said.

"I'll bet we can find time after the guests leave. Perhaps I should ask Daddy about what he thinks of the idea? I don't ever remember him mentioning Mud before."

When we got back to our camp, we unloaded the horses, Sally started supper, and I fed the horses. Sally's supper was a lot better than the noon meal I'd had at Mud's the day before.

"We'd better break camp in the mornin' an' head toward the ranch," I said.

"We could spend an extra day," said Sally. "It isn't often we get a chance to take a vacation in the middle of summer."

"That's temptin'," I said, "but we better get back."

The next morning while Sally did the breakfast dishes, I broke camp. I rolled up our bedrolls and tent. Sally packed the dishes in the cooler and we tied the cooler, bedrolls, and tent to the cab of the truck. I got the pistol from the brush where I'd hid it and put it behind the seat of the truck. We haltered the horses and tied them, head to tail in the truck. The colts were loaded loose. Our summer vacation, if we could call it that, was over.

I got to thinking about Dusty Waters and made up my mind to question Bud about him. He didn't seem too sociable and there was a lot about Bud's past that I didn't know.

A Shady Past?

The trip home was uneventful. I took care not to drive too fast. The horses were crowded in the truck and the colts needed every break they could get in there with the big horses.

It was almost suppertime when we pulled into the ranch. We were met by the ranch hands and most of the guests. Even Bud wheeled himself down to the corral to find out what had happened. We took care of the horses and I told Bud and Pat about the happenings of the last couple of days. I told Jimmy he'd be responsible for the orphaned colt—feeding him and working a little each day to halter break him.

Bud asked, "What about the stud?"

"I came across a cow camp an' the old cowboy there told me he'd shot the stud," I said.

"Really? How come?"

"The old man said the horse acted like he'd lost his head or somethin'. It sounded like brain fever to me," I said. "He gave me the brand off the horse. It's in the truck, it's our brand. He told me he put the horse out of his misery."

"Who was this old cowboy?"

"He said his name was Dusty Waters."

"Mud!" exclaimed Bud. "Hear that Pat? Old Mud's still around. What's that old hermit doing?'

"Apparently he's holed up in a cow camp ridin' fence, scatterin' salt an' the like," I said. "He has a hard time gettin' around."

"I'll bet," said Bud. "He's a tough old bird. You know, he had some knee trouble quite a while ago and never could get it fixed. Finally, he told the doc, 'Either fix it or cut it off!' They couldn't fix it, so they cut it off. Yep. He's about as tough as they come."

"He told Sally he hadn't seen her since she was in diapers," I said.

"It's been a long time since he was around here," said Bud.

"I don't remember you ever talkin' about him before," I said.

"There's really not much to say about him," said Bud. "Back in the days when he, Pat, and I were running around, he almost got us into some real trouble more than once. I remember once when he got Pat thrown into jail."

"Those were trumped up charges and you know it," said Pat, indignantly. "And if you remember I was released the next day, with the apologies from the sheriff."

"But he still had you locked up," said Bud.

"That's right, but it's not on my record. In fact I don't have a record," said Pat. "So I had a free night's sleep at the expense of the city. I'd just as soon forget it, in fact I thought I had until you brought it up."

"That's all in the past," said Bud.

"Of course, you don't remember the fight you and Mud had over a woman, if I remember right," said Pat.

"Certainly, I remember," said Bud, his mood changing from a joking one to a more somber one. "You had to break up that fight, didn't you?"

"Yes," answered Pat. "And I got the worst of it for doing just that."

"By the way," asked Bud, "who won that fight?"

"I don't know," answered Pat, "but I do know that I didn't."

"We haven't seen him since then, have we?"

"No," said Pat. "He left the county and I don't know where he went, although I heard he had become a hermit and lived up in the mountains somewhere. He did come by here a time or two since then."

I asked, "What started the fight?"

"It was a long time ago," said Bud, "before Sally's mother and I

33

were married. Mud had made some remarks about her that weren't too … ah … let's say complimentary. I thought somebody had better do something about it, so I punched him. Well, he retaliated, and the fight was on! At one point, I thought he was going to kill me."

"And I thought Bud was going to kill Mud. That's when I jumped in," said Pat. "And both of them almost killed me!"

"I finally got the upper hand and Mud laid out in the corral, cold-cocked. Pat helped me in the house and doctored my cuts and bruises. I think he broke a couple of ribs—if they weren't broke, they were cracked. I was a long time healing. When Pat got done with me, he went out to get Mud but he was gone."

"He woke up, saddled his horse and rode off," said Pat.

"He did come by a few years later," said Bud, "after Sally was born, and made his amends. I made my apologies and I thought things would be like they were before, but he stayed a few days, played a little with Sally, and then rode off. He hasn't been around since. I really didn't think he'd hold a grudge, but I guess he has."

Bud shook his head in a sad manner. "It's a shame how some people can't forgive and forget," he continued. "I don't like to think it was me that caused him to ride off and live a life of solitude."

I hadn't heard much about the history of the ranch, so I asked, "How'd he get Pat thrown in jail?"

"Mud had gathered some of the neighbor's cows and put them in a corral close to where Pat was camped," said Bud. "The neighbor's hired man saw them, reported it to his boss and the neighbor called the sheriff. The sheriff came out, surveyed the situation and took Pat into custody. It took a lot of talking on Mud's part to get the sheriff to release Pat and he almost got himself thrown into jail doing it."

"Really," I said. "How'd he do that?"

Bud continued, "When Mud found out that Pat had been hauled to jail, he went to the jail the next day. He started out by telling the sheriff that he put the cattle in the corral as a practical joke, knowing the neighbor would call the sheriff. When he saw the sheriff wasn't going to buy that, he told him that he thought the cattle had strayed and he corralled them with the idea that he'd notify the neighbor where the cattle were. The sheriff bought that idea and released Pat."

I asked, "Where were you at the time, Bud?"

"Oh, I was there all right. I was the hired man that told the neighbor his cows were being stolen."

"How come you were workin' for the neighbor?"

Bud answered, "My dad farmed Pat and me out to the neighbor for a few months. He'd had some tough luck and Dad wanted to help him out."

Pat was standing nearby, grinning. "I didn't think it was too funny at the time, but I can laugh at it now," he said. "I still think both you and Mud set up the deal."

"We don't mention that around here," said Bud. "Being a dude outfit, some of the guests might become somewhat apprehensive knowing that a former jailbird was present!" Bud laughed at his comment.

Pat tried to give him a dirty look, but was laughing just the same. Deciding enough had been said about his somewhat shady past, Pat changed the subject by asking, "What are you goin' to do with the orphaned colt?"

"We'll have to keep him in an' give him some extra care," I said. "He's big enough to be weaned, but he'll need some extra handlin'."

"It's not good for a young horse be alone. He needs to be around other horses to learn his manners," said Bud.

"I know," I said. "I might keep one of the other mares an' colt in just to keep him company. We can put 'em in that small pasture on the creek. We'll have to bring 'em in every day to give him some extra feed, but we'll do it. We also need to think about gettin' another stud. We've got too many mares for our other stud to handle."

"We could cull some of our older mares this fall," said Bud. "Having two stud bunches is a pain in the neck."

"That might be the prudent thing to do," I said.

"I'll get with Sally and we'll decide which mares to let go," said Bud. "She's done all the registering and knows the horses as well as anybody. We'll get that done pretty quickly so we can include them in the sale catalog."

"By the way," interjected Sally, "Mud kinda hinted he could use some help getting a maverick bull captured. Do you have any objection to us going down there to help him out?"

"I don't think so," answered Bud. "There's no reason we can't be neighborly, as long as it doesn't take all summer."

"I was thinking in the fall after the dudes have left," said Sally.

"That's even better," exclaimed Bud.

The discussion about Mud and the earlier days prodded my curiosity about Bud and Pat's earlier years. I decided to pry into it when I could. Later that night, I asked Sally about the past.

"I don't know much about it," she said. "But if you get the chance, you might ask Pat to tell you about Daddy learning how to drive a car. It's hilarious!"

"But you can tell me, can't you?"

"I'd rather have Pat tell you, he was there. Make sure Daddy is around when he tells you, it's a little embarrassing for him, but I think he enjoys it."

The next day, I cornered Pat and asked him to tell me about Bud learning how to drive a car.

"Are you sure you want to do that to Bud? I like to tell it when there's a big group of people around," said Pat. "It's sorta fun to see Bud a little embarrassed."

"My curiosity is aroused," I said. "I need to hear the story."

"Well, I'll tell it at the next dance we have, it's always good for a laugh."

I normally didn't care for the dances we held for the guests, but couldn't wait until Friday when we'd scheduled the next one. I didn't figure myself to be much of a dancer, but Sally said I was getting better. I went mainly because I considered it to be part of my job on the ranch. And I always remembered how my mother taught me how to dance in the kitchen. I had to pay her for this duty by doing the dishes every night.

Mother had always said, "He did learn how to dance pretty well, but the real benefit he got out of it was that his hands were cleaner than they had been in years from doing all those dishes!" She always laughed at her comment.

Friday finally arrived and after supper all the guests gathered in

36

the recreation room for the dance. My first year at the ranch, music was supplied by the hired help, but the last few years Sally had hired a local band to come out and play every other week. I think they played for their supper and a little gas money as they always showed up in time for supper. They only played for a couple of hours as everyone that worked on the ranch got up early. Some, but not all of the guests also got up early.

When the band took a break, Sally took the microphone and announced, "During our break, Pat has a story to tell you. So get your drinks, gather around and don't go away!"

Pat took the stage, put a chair in front of the microphone and said, "I'm going to tell you how Bud Wilson learned how to drive a car. You'll have to imagine me as Bud and it's the first time he's been in a car. Now, some of the language he uses is quite colorful and not really suitable for all family members, so when he uses this language, I'll just say 'Blankety blank!' You can fill in what cuss words you feel appropriate for the situation.

"Bud decided to look into buying one of them new cars that were becoming popular, so he went to the dealership to try one out. The salesman looked at him rather suspiciously, and with some apprehension took him to a demo car. Bud's never been in a car before, he'd always drove a horse drawn wagon. So, rather than opening the door, he climbs over the door of the convertible. This may have been a mistake in judgment because on the way he got one of his spurs caught on the door and he fell into the car. We could hear him saying, 'How do you get in this blankety blank?' as he was falling. He got himself straightened around and I heard him muttering, 'That's a blankety blank of a thing, I got bucked off the blankety blank before I even got on.' When he got himself righted I heard him say, 'Get up! Get moving fellers!'

"The salesman looked more apprehensive as he pointed out the brake and clutch. 'I don't think you'll need those,' he said pointing to Bud's spurs.

"Then Bud asked, pointing at the floor, 'What are they for?'

"The salesman told him, 'The brake is for stopping and the clutch is for shifting gears.'

37

"Bud said, 'I know what a brakes for. What do you think I am, an idiot? What's a clutch?'

"The salesman was very patient and said, 'The clutch is for moving. You push in that pedal on the left and I'll work the gearshift until you get the hang of it. The pedal on the right is the brake.'"

Pat had the crowd laughing and I hadn't realized what an entertainer he was. I was enjoying the story, too.

Pat continued, "Bud clucked to the car again, just as he would to a team of horses pulling a wagon, but he didn't get any response. 'How do you get this blankety blank thing moving?' The salesman, his patience wearing a little thin, said, 'You turn the key, here on the dashboard, then push that little button, the starter, on the floor, between the gas pedal and the brake.' Bud started to reach down to the button on the floor with his hand, but the salesman stopped him. 'No, sir! You push the starter with your foot!'

"Bud did as he was told and the car started. Bud jumped as the engine started. 'The blankety blank thing is growling at me!'

"The salesman told Bud, 'Now push in the clutch, I'll put it in gear and you let out on the clutch, slowly. Give it a little gas, that's the gas pedal on the floor between the brake and the starter button.'

"Bud did as he was told and the car jumped forward. 'Guess I let out the blankety blank clutch too fast!' 'Yes,' said the salesman. 'This blankety blank car is very responsive.'

"Bud was very trying on the salesman and the salesman was beginning to cuss!"

Pat had the crowd laughing as they pictured in their minds Bud trying to drive the vehicle. Pat's physical motions and facial expressions as he narrated the story only added to the comedy. I understood why Sally had insisted Pat tell the story. I looked at Bud and he was enjoying the story although he looked a little embarrassed.

Pat continued, "The car was bouncing forward as Bud let up on the gas, then depressed it. 'This blankety blank is trying to buck!' hollered Bud. The salesman had already jumped out of the car and was running alongside, shouting instructions to Bud. 'I'm trying to stop the blankety blank thing,' Bud was hollering back.'

"Now picture this. Bud was pulling back on the steering wheel as hard as he could, hollering, 'Whoa, you blankety blank, whoa!' At the same time he was pulling back on the steering wheel, he was pressing his feet as hard as he could on the floorboard, as he would with a runaway team and wagon. The only problem was that his right foot was on the gas pedal, so the harder he pulled and pressed, the faster he went. And he was yelling, 'Whoa, you blankety blank, whoa!' the whole time.

"The owner of the dealership saw what was happening and came running out of the building, jumped on the running board of the car, and dove into the front seat head first. I heard him mutter something about 'those blankety blank cowboys!' as he turned off the key.

"Bud got out of the car the same way he got in, over the door. 'Those blankety blank things are sure blankety blanks to handle!'

"The salesman regained some of his composure and said, 'Yes, they are blankety blanks! I don't think you're quite ready for a car, sir!'

"Bud allowed as to he might not be ready for a car at this time and we left with Bud muttering something about those 'blankety blank cars' and the salesman and the owner were muttering something about those 'blankety blank cowboys!'"

All the guests were enjoying the story as Pat got ready to leave the stage. They gave him a nice round of applause as he left.

Bud hollered, "You folks don't want to believe everything you hear from that old waddy!"

One of the guests asked Pat, "What do you call your story?"

"I don't know," replied Pat. "I guess I'll call it my blankety blank story."

This brought another laugh from the guests and some more applause.

The band returned and the dance continued. After a dance with Sally, I cornered Pat and asked him, "How much of that story is true?"

"It's all true, my boy. It's all true! You didn't hear Bud try to correct me, did you? You know he's too honest not to correct me if I was stretching the truth."

39

Peaceful Days

The rest of the summer was going well. The dude rides were going every day and were peaceful. We did a branding every week or ten days, just to give the dudes some real cowboy action, in spite of the fact that the calves needed branding. Jimmy was kept a little busier taking care of the orphaned colt, but he didn't seem to mind.

I asked him one day, "Is takin' care of the colt gettin' to be too much for you?"

"Nope," replied Jimmy. "In fact it's kinda nice to be working with him all alone."

"Well," I said, "if it gets a little tiresome, you can have Blake, Quince, or Devin give you a hand. I gave you the job because I knew you could handle it an' do a good job of it. You've shown a lot of responsibility on this job an' I know I appreciate it. I know Sally an' Bud appreciate it as much as I do."

Although the peaceful atmosphere was just what a dude ranch like ours wanted and needed, I was becoming restless. There was plenty of riding on the dude rides, even though it was all at a walk, and occasionally when we gathered cattle for the brandings, we'd have to run after a cow, but it was becoming mundane. Every now and then one of the colts we'd started offered to buck, but we could generally ease him out of it.

Blake was riding one of the colts at a branding when the colt offered to buck and the colt bucked Blake off. Blake wasn't much of a bronc rider, although he professed to be and wanted to be. He got his rope under the colt's tail and he started to buck. The colt didn't buck hard and Blake could have pulled his head up fairly easily, but decided to let him go. When Blake hit the ground, he tried to brace himself with his hands and I think that's where he broke his wrist. He claimed the colt stepped on his wrist, and he could have, but I didn't see it.

As Blake got up, holding his right wrist and trying to fight back the tears, all the guests gathered around him to see how he was and if he was hurt. I had to smile at Blake's effort to hold back the tears—I'd broken some bones before and knew how painful it was. Everyone was asking him, at the same time, "Are you all right?"

Blake's answer was a simple, painful, "I think I sprained my wrist."

One of the guests, a Mister Goodrich, made his way through the dudes gathered around Blake. "Let me through," he said, "I'm a doctor!"

Doctor Goodrich examined Blake's wrist, not without some additional pain to Blake.

"It's just a sprain, Doc," exclaimed Blake. "It'll be all right in a couple of days!"

"No," replied Doctor Goodrich, "I believe it's broken. Somebody needs to take this boy to the hospital where he can be X-rayed and have it set properly."

"But it's just a bad sprain," reaffirmed Blake. "It'll be all right in a couple of days!"

"You'd better go to town and have it looked at properly," said Doctor Goodrich. "If you don't, you might end up not having it heal correctly and lose much of the use of your right hand. You could end up partially handicapped for the rest of your life."

Bud, who had been sitting outside the corral observing the branding, hollered, "What's the diagnosis?"

"It's broke," I hollered back. "The Doc here says he needs to go to town to the hospital."

"Okay," said Bud. "Get him in the golf cart. Jimmy, you come along, you and I can take him to town."

"I don't have anything to immobilize that wrist with," said Doctor Goodrich. "It's important to keep it immobilized."

Devin asked, "Will this wild rag help?"

"Possibly," replied the doctor. "We'll need some sticks or something to use as a splint to keep it from moving."

A search was made for something solid to use as a splint and the best anyone could come up with was some fairly solid sagebrush limbs.

"This is the best we could come up with," said someone, as he handed the limbs to the doctor.

"It'll have to do," said the doctor, as he took the sagebrush and wild rag and made a splint for Blake's wrist.

As he tied the wild rag around the splint, the doctor said, "That's not very professional, but it will have to do under the circumstances. Son," he said to Blake, "you keep this immobile. Don't move it at all."

Blake made his way to the golf cart where Bud was already waiting and got on. As Jimmy got on, he said to Devin, "Be sure to take care of my orphaned colt and take my horse in and take care of him."

"Sure," said Devin.

"I'll take care of your horse, Blake," said Quince.

Before Bud, Jimmy, and Blake headed out, Bud told Sally, "We might be in town for a day or two. I'll get a room at the hotel and Jimmy can stay at his folk's house. I'll call you tonight and let you know what's going on."

Sally's reply was a simple, "Okay."

Someone asked, "Why did that happen?"

Pat replied, "The horse decided to buck and Blake just let him. He could have stopped him, but he let him go. The horse got the best of him."

"Some of our young college student hands have aspirations of being top notch bronc riders," I said. "Did you see how his right hand went up when the colt started to buck? I guess Blake thought he was in a rodeo arena ridin' for money."

"What started the horse to bucking?"

"That's a young horse," I replied. "He hasn't been ridden as much as the older horses an' he's not used to the unexpected. Blake

42

got his rope under the horse's tail. An' that area under a horse's tail is kinda sensitive. Blake should have stopped him. It's not good to let these young horses buck. They might find that they like it, then you've got a problem. Buckin' might be the only thing they want to do. I'll ride the horse the next couple of days, just to make sure the colt doesn't want to make a lifelong profession of bucking. I'm sure Bud will give a similar talk to Blake on the way to town. He wasn't too pleased with what happened and the results."

"Bud didn't appear to be upset with Blake. What will happen to Blake? Will he be fired?"

It was clear the guests were concerned with Blake and his injury. He did get along well with the guests and was a likeable young man.

"Bud's pretty good at hidin' his feelin's," I said. "Blake won't lose his job. We'll bring him back from the hospital an' use him where we can, although a one-armed man ain't much help. That's just the chapter on accidents, don't let it affect you. It comes with the job an' it's always possible."

We continued the branding. Sally gave up her turn at roping and went around to each guest and tried to console those that were visibly affected by Blake's misfortune. She seemed to be successful, as everyone's mood was visibly better after a time.

When she had reassured everyone, she came to me and said, "Every one of the hands seems to be getting along well. Did you see the way Jimmy told Devin to take care of his horse? And how Quince volunteered to take care of Blake's horse?"

"Yes," I replied, "they all get along well."

We finished the branding and moved the cows and calves to the next pasture. Before we started back to the ranch, I sent Devin and Quince back for Blake and Jimmy's horses.

"Just go to the ranch fellers," I said. "You shouldn't get lost," I added jokingly. "I'll send Chuck with you, he knows the way!"

Later that night after supper, Sally got a call from Bud. He told her that they might be in town a day or two longer. Blake's wrist was definitely broken and they'd have to wait until the swelling went down to reset the broken bones.

"Broken bones?" I heard Sally question.

43

Apparently Bud told her there was more than one broken bone and if Blake needed surgery, they'd be longer getting back to the ranch.

Sally's reply was a simple, "Okay, keep me informed."

Sally told me of her conversation with Bud and said, "You need to tell everyone about what's happening."

"Me? Why me?"

"Because you're the boss and the guests need to be informed from the head man."

The next morning at breakfast, Sally said, "Honey has an announcement to make concerning Blake."

There was an audible gasp from the guests as if they expected the worst.

I stood up to make the announcement. "Apparently, Doctor Goodrich's diagnosis of Blake's condition yesterday was correct. Blake did break his wrist."

Everyone applauded the announcement of Doctor Goodrich's diagnosis.

I continued. "Blake has broken more than one bone in his wrist an' a determination will be made as to whether or not surgery will be needed when the swelling goes down."

Again applause came from the guests.

"There is no need for concern," I continued. "Blake is under a doctor's care an' should be all right. It's only a broken wrist. It's not a life threatening situation an' it's a long way from his heart!"

A laugh erupted from the guests.

"Blake, Bud, an' Jimmy should be back in a couple of days. There is no need for concern. Just go ahead an' enjoy your vacation, we'll continue here as though nothing happened," I concluded.

Another round of applause came from the guests as I sat down.

"That was a very good impromptu talk you gave. I didn't know you were a public speaker," said Sally.

"I ain't," I replied.

"But you did much better than I could have done. You have talents I didn't even know you had."

"This job brings out unexpected talents in a person," I said as modestly as I could. "I personally felt like there was too much concern over Blake's accident and I felt like everyone should enjoy their vacation."

"You're absolutely correct," complimented Sally. "By the way, I think I'm pregnant again!"

I was totally shocked and surprised. All I could say was, "As I said, this job brings out unexpected talents in a person!" I gave Sally a big hug and told her how happy I was.

Sally smiled and didn't say anything.

Two days later, about noon, Bud, Jimmy, and Blake returned to the ranch. Everyone greeted them and almost mercilessly asked how Blake was doing. Blake enjoyed the attention and Bud called Doctor Goodrich.

Bud said, "The doc at the hospital said I should tell you that was an excellent job of splinting Blake's wrist, although somewhat primitive and ..."

"Somewhat primitive!" exclaimed Doctor Goodrich. "I did as good as I could with what I had to work with!"

Bud continued, "The doc said that your splint job probably prevented his having to operate."

"That's what I'd hoped for," said the good doctor.

"Our worker's comp will handle Blake's medical bill," said Bud, "but what do we owe you for your services? Name any figure you want, I'll deduct it from of Blake's wages."

The doctor and Bud both laughed. Pat and I laughed also. Blake showed some dismay when Bud said he'd take the bill out of his wages.

"I wouldn't worry about it," said the doctor.

"But Doctor Goodrich," said Bud, "you made a house call and not too many doctors make house calls these days. Besides that, you made it on a horse and it's been quite a few years since any doctor made a house call on horseback!"

Seeing that Bud was having a good time at Blake's expense, the doctor decided to join the fun. "You're absolutely right! This could be a fairly expensive little venture! I'll have to give it some serious consideration."

Blake showed more dismay at the doctor's comment.

Seeing Blake's dismay at the situation, Bud said, "It's about time for the noon meal. Devin, you and Quince gather up the preserves Jimmy's mother sent out and take them to the kitchen."

"I'll give you a hand," said Jimmy.

We continued our chores the rest of the week with Blake doing what he could with his wrist in a cast. When it came time for Doctor Goodrich and his family to leave, I saw Blake saying goodbye to the doctor. At the same time, I saw him reaching for his wallet. I decided to question him about it when we had a spare minute, but we didn't have time now. Guests were leaving and some new guests were arriving.

The next morning after we had run in the horses and were saddling them, I asked Blake, "What did the doctor charge you for the house call?"

"He didn't charge me anything. I offered to pay him, but he said, 'Just a thanks son, just a thanks.' Did Bud pay him?"

"Not that I know of," I said. "I think he offered, but the doc refused. You got some free medical care."

"I'm sure appreciative of it," said Blake.

I rode Blake's horse and didn't have any trouble with him, although I was careful to keep my rope from under his tail. The horse was careful also, eyeing it suspiciously and trying to side step it as I coiled up. Because of Blake's experience at the branding, I roped off his horse at the brandings we held the rest of the summer. The horse had a lot of respect for the rope and even side stepped it when I threw it to catch a calf. Consequently, I missed a lot of throws.

Sally noticed this one day and assessing the situation, said, "Honey, maybe you ought to use my horse for roping. You seem to be missing a lot of throws."

"I appreciate the offer, Darlin'," I said, "but the horse needs the experience. An' the way I'm ropin', I need the experience, too!"

I spent a lot of time during the summer riding Blake's horse and letting my rope drag on the ground to get the horse accustomed to the rope. It took a lot of doing, but the horse finally stopped trying to side step the rope as I coiled it. And he stopped ducking away when I would throw it. My roping seemed to be getting better, although nobody said anything. I was a little disappointed that nobody noticed, but I didn't start bragging that my roping was improving.

The summer wore on. There wasn't anything happening that was especially noteworthy, everything went well. Sally took Blake in to have his wrist checked and also set up appointments to have her pregnancy monitored. She took Ginny on these trips and they enjoyed doing some shopping. I think they enjoyed the ice cream cones that came at the end of the trip more than the shopping. When they'd get home, they'd tell me how much they liked the ice cream.

I asked, "How come you didn't bring me any?"

Ginny answered, "We did, Daddy. But it started to melt and Mommy told me to eat it before it made a mess all over the car!"

"I don't believe that," I said.

"Well, it's true Daddy," said Ginny.

"True! Can you prove that?"

"I can," said Ginny.

"How?"

"Daddy, there's no ice cream left and there isn't any ice cream all over the car. I did what Mommy told me to," said Ginny.

I have to admit, my own daughter had me there!

Maybe Too Much Action?

The summer wore on and for the most part, it was very peaceful. Our rides were relaxing and safe. One day, Pat came to me and said, "You startin' to get a little restless?"

I didn't think it showed and certainly tried to hide it, but I had to answer Pat honestly. "I guess so," I said. "I didn't think it showed."

"Well, it happens to everyone this time of year," said Pat. "A little bit of boredom, the same trails, the same country, the same horses, and the same people all week. It even happened to Bud, but he overcame it. I'm starting to feel it a little myself."

I asked, "What'd Bud do to overcome it?"

"Back in the old days, Bud used to go get entered in some rodeos. That seemed to help, but he tired of it, or got too old. I think he started looking forward to new dudes arriving and trying to see what new jokes or stunts he could pull on them. That seems to help."

"What do you do for it?"

"Nothin'," replied Pat. "The summer will soon be over and the monotony will change."

"I'm thinkin' I might want to go down an' see if I can capture that wild bull Dusty Waters was talkin' about," I said. "That might be kinda adventuresome."

"You can count on me," said Pat. "Jimmy and Sally will want to go. Bud might even want to go down and visit with old Mud."

"We can't take everybody," I said. "Somebody needs to stay home an' keep an eye on things. Our summer wranglers, Quince,

Devin, an' Blake will be leavin' for school before long. Chuck wants to move on. Something about seein' an old girlfriend."

"Jimmy could handle things when there are fewer dudes around," said Pat.

"Most of the dudes will be gone right after Labor Day," I said. "We might be able to slip away for a few days then. I'm kinda lookin' forward to it. If nothin' else comes up, lets plan on it. I'll talk to Sally. After Labor Day is when Chuck wants to leave."

"Good," said Pat. "If that bull's as wild as Mud says he is, we'll need our best horses. I'll start gettin' some things together. That might be good for a change, and I'd like to see how Mud's doing."

The thought of doing some real cowboying in the near future just seemed to make the days drag on. But finally, a few days after Labor Day, the majority of the dudes had left. There were just a few guests on the ranch. Sally was preparing to move to town so Ginny could start school. She would come out on weekends and help, but she felt like her obligations to her daughter and her daughter's education were important. I'm sure Missus Abercrombie had something to do with that.

Devin and Blake had left to return to school. Quince didn't have to be back to school for another week so he stayed longer. Most of the maids we'd hired also had to return to school, but two of them were able to stay longer. Jimmy didn't have to go back to school until the winter semester began and he was going to stay until New Year's. My sister Betty had also left to return to school.

We made preparations to go hunt down the wild bull. As I gathered some things, I made a mental inventory of the help that would be left at the ranch. Bud would be there and even from his wheelchair, he could supervise the day-to-day operations of the ranch. I checked the reservation board and there weren't so many guests expected to arrive that it would overload the help. There were two maids left and Missus Abercrombie could supervise them and even do a little of the work herself.

Knowing that Missus Abercrombie wouldn't be able to do much work, I called a lady in town to see if she could come out and give us a hand for a few days. We'd hired the woman before and she was available to work for a few days. Contented that the ranch and the dudes could be taken care of, Pat and I loaded two each of our best horses in the two-ton truck, packed enough groceries to last a week, and put our bedrolls in the truck. We headed out, with me driving.

When we got well past the boundaries of the ranch, Pat made the comment, "It's been quite a few years since I've been down here. I don't remember much of this country."

"We've got a long way to go before we get to Dusty Waters place," I said. "An' it'll be slow goin' from here on out. This ain't much of a road."

"Ol' Mud always said he wanted to get as far away from civilization as he could," said Pat. "Looks to me that he's about done it."

"He does have an old truck he can use to get to town. I saw it when I was down here before."

"Yeah, he probably only goes to town once, maybe twice a year," said Pat.

"I wonder how he gets along all year."

"He does all right, I suspect. He was always pretty resourceful."

We lumbered along what was supposed to be a road, mostly in silence. My thoughts were mostly about how Mud got along during the year. I surmised he probably ate a lot of venison, perhaps an elk, maybe some beef he'd killed. It seemed like a fairly simple existence to me.

Along the way, we spotted some cows, but they were too far off to see any brands on them. "We'll tell Mud about those cows," said Pat. "Although I suspect he already knows."

When we arrived at Mud's, the day was pretty well over. It wasn't dark yet, but it wouldn't be long before it was. The wild horses and donkey Sally and I had left when we came looking for the stud were in a little pasture next to the corrals. They were all hobbled.

Mud wasn't present when we showed up, but we unloaded our horses, put them in the corral and threw them some hay. Presently we saw Mud making his way down the slope off a small ridge. He was carrying a shovel over his shoulder and seemed to be limping. When he reached fairly level ground, the limp disappeared.

He was eying us carefully as he approached and his look of suspicion disappeared when he recognized us.

"If it ain't Pat!" His exclamation held a tone of surprise. "Where you been hidin' all these years?"

They shook hands vigorously and patted each other on the back. I was surprised they didn't hug. It was plain they had known each other well in the past. There was a lot of animation in their conversation.

"I've been up at Bud's. You know Honey here, don't you?"

"Yeah, I met him awhile back when he was lookin' for his lost horses. How you doing, sonny?"

"Fine," I replied, feeling like an intruder at a family reunion.

Turning to Pat, and not waiting for my reply, Mud said, "So you been up at Bud's all these years, huh? How come you ain't been down for a visit?"

"I didn't know you were here. You ain't been much good at keeping in touch. And you knew where Bud was, how come you ain't been up to say hello?"

"You know me," said Mud, "I ain't much good in a crowd and when I'd heard Bud turned his outfit into a dude ranch, I just didn't feel the need to go up there. But I have thought a lot about you guys."

"But not enough to come up for a visit," said Pat.

I couldn't tell if the reunion was turning a little sour or not.

"Since I got this artificial leg, I don't get around much," said Mud.

Pat asked, "What's the shovel for?"

"I been doing a little gardening and irrigating," said Mud. "Come in the house, I'll fix us up something to eat. Bring your bedrolls."

"We've got some groceries in the truck, we'll bring 'em," said Pat.

"Probably canned stuff," replied Mud. "Not near as good as my home grown."

"You might be right," said Pat, "but we'll bring 'em in anyways. There's some meat in the cooler."

"Bring it if you must, but I've got some fresh venison in there."

"You ain't been poaching, have you?" Pat asked facetiously.

Eying me suspiciously, Mud answered, "Nope, I ain't been poaching. I was out doing some target practicing, and doing real well, when this fat forked-horn buck, still in the velvet, stepped right in my line of fire. He went down and by the time I got there, he was already dead. There wasn't anything I could do to save him, so I cut his throat, gutted him, and brought him home. I didn't think he should go to waste even if he wanted to commit suicide!"

Pat and I laughed. "Still got that old line of bull!" said Pat.

"That's the way it happened," said Mud. "Here, I'll give you a hand packing that stuff in."

We started toward the house carrying bedrolls and groceries. Inside the house, Mud said, "There's a spare room over there with a couple of beds in it, put your bedrolls in there."

I wasn't surprised at the inside of Mud's house. It was cluttered and messy, much like I'd expect an old bachelor's house to be, and I'd been in it before. But the spare room was worse. It seemed to be a place where Mud had collected his junk.

I told Pat, "I'll clean this stuff off the beds, if you want to finish unloading the groceries an' continue your reunion with Mud."

Pat looked around the room, kinda disgustedly, and said, "Good. I'd kinda forgot what a lousy housekeeper Mud was."

I started moving stuff off the beds and trying to clear a pathway to them. As I worked, I could hear them talking, reliving the old days. There was a lot of laughter interjected into their conversation and I could tell that they'd spent a lot of time together in the past.

Their conversation eventually turned to Bud and the Wilson Ranch. Pat told how turning the ranch into a dude operation saved the ranch and that we had three aspects on the ranch that provided income: the dudes, the cattle, and the registered horses.

"I saw the stud," said Mud. "In fact, I shot him!"

"I know," said Pat, "Honey told us about it."

"The horse needed it. There wasn't nothin' I could do. Brain fever or something like that. He looked like a mighty fine horse," said Mud.

"He was," replied Pat. "His colts had a lot of color and they were built real well. It'll be hard to replace him. We've got another stud, younger, and he seems to show a lot of promise. Bud will probably cull some of the older mares and just have one stud bunch in the future."

Mud asked, "You mean he's been running two stud bunches?"

"Up until you shot his stud," answered Pat.

They both laughed. Then Mud said, "When Bud culls his mares, I'd like to get one or two of 'em. My horses are showing some age and I'll have to start thinking about replacing them before long. If I could get a couple of pregnant mares, I'd be in pretty good shape. I could break the colts and have something decent to ride."

"They'd be spotted colts," said Pat.

"You know me," said Mud, "I don't much care about color. Them horses you put in the corral look to be pretty good horses."

"Honey and I brought a couple of our best horses to capture your maverick bull," said Pat.

"He's a wild one," said Mud. "You remember that cow that got snowed in that box canyon one winter? She survived, but she came out as wild and crazy as anythin' could be. She was a handful to handle. That bull is worse. He's put me and my horses on the run more than once. I wondered if my old horses could outrun him."

"Our horses can outrun him," said Pat. "Do you know where he's hangin' out?"

"Not exactly," replied Mud, "but I got a pretty good idea. We can go look for him in the morning."

"Where are your horses?"

"My horses are hobbled," replied Mud. "They shouldn't be far. They'll probably be in for grain in the morning."

"Good! You got supper ready yet?"

"It'll be a few more minutes. Tell Honey to get ready, it won't be long."

We ate a supper of venison steaks and Pat and Mud continued their reunion. I was mostly ignored, but enjoyed the steak.

After supper, I continued to straighten up the spare room while

53

Pat and Mud carried on their conversation. Soon, I came out of the spare room and said, "It's been a rough day for me, all that drivin' an' cleanin' up. I'm ready to hit the sack."

Pat said, "We'll try to locate that bull in the morning. Then with a little luck, we can gather those cows we saw, move them toward the bull and maybe put all of 'em in a corral."

"That might work," said Mud. "But that bull's pretty smart. He's good at staying out of corrals."

"That's the best I can come up with. You got any ideas, Honey?"

"Nope," I answered. "We'll try that an' see how good it works."

We spent the next day looking for the bull. It was very similar to our dude rides, although Pat and Mud did a lot of talking about things that weren't considered to be good conversational topics around the dudes. I enjoyed that myself.

We located the bull on a hillside off in the distance a mile or so. We didn't approach him—Mud assured us it was him.

"There's a good set of corrals about a mile and a half down that valley," said Mud.

"Good," said Pat. "Tomorrow, we'll bring the cows up here and leave 'em in the valley overnight so the bull can get acquainted with 'em. The next day, we'll start 'em all toward the corral. Hopefully, we can corral 'em all. Does that sound good to you, Honey?"

"Sounds like a plan to me," I said.

"When we start them toward the corrals, we don't want to rush 'em," said Mud. "We'll just take our time. We need to work the cattle from a distance so we don't spook the bull."

Pat asked, "Can we move the cattle from where they are to over here legally?"

"Don't see why not," answered Mud, "they're my cows."

We rode back to Mud's place, confident that our plan for the next couple of days would succeed. On the way we passed a garden about half an acre in size. I figured it was Mud's garden. I was surprised. There wasn't a weed in sight. It was neat and clean and showed all the signs of being taken care of by an expert gardener. There was a six-foot high fence all around the garden. I was really surprised as I looked at the garden and compared it to Mud's house. I wondered, *How could a person keep such a neat garden and let his house be in a shambles?*

Mud saw my astonishment and said, "The fence is to keep out the deer and elk."

Mud mistook my amazement—I knew what an elk fence was, but I didn't say anything.

Pat and Mud continued to visit between themselves and totally ignored me. We got back to Mud's cabin, took care of our horses, and Mud fixed supper. There wasn't anything for me to do other than sit back and relax. I didn't need the relaxing, I hadn't done anything other than ride a slow dude ride without any dudes.

The next morning we rounded up the cattle and herded them to the little valley where we'd spotted the bull. There was only about thirty head of cows and their calves. I noticed that the calves seemed to be of all ages, evidence that the bull had been at work year round. It took us all day, but we got all the cattle to the valley.

The next morning, as we were saddling our horses, Mud made the suggestion, "Why don't we truck our horses to the corrals? We can unload 'em there and ride around the ridge, get behind the cattle, and start 'em toward the corrals. It'll save a lot of time."

That was a good suggestion, but I wasn't sure if Mud made it to save time or because his artificial leg was giving him problems. I'd noticed a more pronounced limp when he got off his horse the afternoon before.

"That sounds like a good idea to me," I said. "Let's do it."

We loaded the horses in the truck and started out. At the corrals, we unloaded the horses, tightened the cinches and set out. An hour later, we topped the ridge that lined the valley. It didn't take long before we spotted the cattle and the bull was with them. So far, our plan had worked one hundred percent.

Slowly, without any yelling, we started the cattle toward the corrals. Everything was going smoothly, better than we had expected or even hoped for.

About three hours later, the corrals were in sight. Shortly, a few of the cows and calves entered the corral. Mud urged his horse a little closer to the corrals. When the bull entered the corral, Mud ran as fast as his horse could go, rushing the cattle. When Pat and I saw him speed up, we spurred our horses as fast as we could get to the corrals.

"I'll get the gate," hollered Mud as he entered the corral. Mud leaped off his horse, lit standing, which surprised me for a one-legged man, and got the gate closed and latched. Then he had to climb the gate to keep from getting gored by the bull. The bull heard him and wheeled around toward the gate. Mud got over the gate just in time, leaving his horse in the corral. The bull saw the horse and immediately took after him and the horse was in full flight from the bull around the corral. The bull was quickly gaining on the horse and as they ran, the bull gored Mud's horse in the flank.

Pat and I were outside the corral, taking our ropes down, hoping to rope the bull before he did any more damage. It was difficult to rope over the corral fence and catch the bull and Pat and I missed our first loops, the ropes just falling on the bull's back.

When the bull felt the ropes on his back, he changed direction, and seeing the opening leading up to the chute, ran at full speed up the chute and into the truck. He didn't stop at the front of the truck, he tried to jump it. Even going at full speed, he couldn't jump high enough to clear the front rack. He busted it and kept going, busting the windshield as he went. He dented the hood as he went over the truck, and kept going.

Pat and I were on the wrong side of the corrals to try and get our ropes on him and we watched him run off at full speed. We turned our attention to Mud, who was looking at his gored horse. The bull had left a gash in the flank of the horse and the horse's intestines were starting to roll out.

"I think I can save him," said Mud. "I've got to get back to the cabin and get some sewing materials. Drive me back, Pat. Honey, you stay here and keep the horse still. Don't let any more of his guts spill out!"

Pat and Mud left, not taking the time to clean the broken glass from the seat of the truck. I was left with a horse that had been gored. I wondered, *How can I keep his guts where they belong?* Then I had an idea.

If I could get something to help keep the intestines inside the belly cavity, it might help. But what? If I had a gunny sack, that might work. Then, I had an idea. My raincoat! It might work perfectly, being made of rubber, and being tied on the back of my saddle, it would certainly be cleaner than a gunny sack.

I got my raincoat from my saddle. Immediately I saw that it was too big. I cut it and took the cleanest portion to the horse. Carefully, I jammed the intestines back into the body cavity, and carefully pressed the raincoat inside. I hoped it would keep the intestines from coming out any farther. It would help if I could keep the horse from moving. That was all I could do until Pat and Mud came back. I was hoping the horse wouldn't die before they arrived.

About two and a half hours later, Pat and Mud showed up, driving Mud's pickup.

The horse had lain down and I figured it was okay. He wouldn't move much being prostate on the ground.

"Keep him down, Honey! I'll be right there," yelled Mud, as he hobbled toward me. "Is he still alive?"

"Yep," I said, "but I don't give him much of a chance."

Mud didn't say anything, but poured a canteen full of water on the wound. Then he went right to starting to sew up the wound. He was working from the horse's back and presently exclaimed, "What's this?!"

"My raincoat," I answered.

"What's it doing here?"

"It was the only way I could think of to keep his guts from coming out," I answered.

"Good thinking," answered Mud, as he pulled the raincoat from inside the horse. Mud looked at the half of the coat and added, "It ain't very big. Looks like it would only keep half of you dry. It's a good thing you used your raincoat, all this water might have done some more harm."

Mud could talk and work at the same time and his attempts at humor during a serious action didn't fall on deaf ears.

"I had to cut it in half," I replied. "But it worked, if infection doesn't set in."

"We'll handle that," said Mud. "I also brought some penicillin."

I hadn't noticed, but Pat had disappeared.

I asked, "Where's Pat?"

"He had another job to do," replied Mud. "He'll be back shortly."

I watched as Mud sewed up the wound, making the stitches real close. When he got done sewing, he filled a syringe full of penicillin and injected it into the horse. Then he gave him another dose. "Hit 'em hard the first shot, then follow it up with regular medication. That's what the vets always told me," he said.

"I'll have to leave the horse here and bring feed and water to him," continued Mud.

In the distance, I heard a sharp sound then a rumbling echo, like thunder. "What's that? Rain comin'?"

Mud looked at the sky. "That's not thunder. That's Pat, doin' his little chore," said Mud.

"Little chore?"

"Yep," replied Mud. "He just killed the bull."

"What with?"

"He used my rifle, the one I use for target practice," answered Mud with a grin.

"I don't see my horse," I said. "I better go hunt him up."

"He was with Pat's horse, over that little rise, when we drove up. He won't be too far."

"I didn't hobble him in all the excitement, what with your horse gettin' gored an' all. I hope he ain't headed for home."

"You hunt up your horse and I'll turn these cows loose," said Mud. "Pat should be back shortly."

I found my horse and much to my surprise, he was hobbled. I didn't remember hobbling him when I got off to see how badly Mud's horse was hurt. I didn't think much of it, took off the hobbles, got on and rode back to the corrals.

"You've got your horse," said Mud when I arrived. "You might want to go out and give Pat a hand. When you find him, light a sagebrush fire so I can use the smoke to find you in the truck. I imagine if Pat's as good a shot as he used to be, he's busy skinnin' and guttin' the bull. Don't want to let him go to waste!"

I rode off in the direction the bull had taken, hoping I could track Pat's horse and find him. I did find him and he had the bull halfway gutted out.

I got off my horse, hobbled him, and started to help Pat. About all I could do was hold a leg out of the way while he brought the intestines, stomach, and lungs out.

"How'd you like fresh liver for supper tonight?"

"I believe I could go for that," I said. "But at the rate the sun's goin' down, it'll be breakfast!"

"It'll go faster now that you're here. And Mud will be here shortly."

"Oh, I got to build a fire so Mud can find us! I almost forgot," I said.

"No need to build a fire, he's coming now. He wasn't that far behind you."

I wondered if Mud wanted a fire so he could find us or if he wanted to get something to eat.

I asked Pat, "Did you hobble my horse before you left? I don't remember hobbling him in the excitement."

"Yep," answered Pat. "He started to follow me when I left, so I hobbled him."

"I appreciate it," I said.

Pat, Mud, and I finished butchering the bull. I was surprised that Mud had skinning knives and a saw in the truck, but then I remembered we'd eaten fresh venison the night before. We quartered the carcass and put it in the truck. The bull wasn't too old—some of the steaks might be a little tough, but Mud could get plenty of hamburger and stew meat.

"That's a job we should have done the first thing when we saw the bull," said Mud. "If we'd have shot him earlier, we wouldn't have a crippled horse or a busted truck. I wish I'd have thought of it earlier."

"Well, it's over now," said Pat. "We'll load up our horses in the morning and head back to the ranch. While this has been fun and it's good to see you, we still have work to do back home."

Mud drove his truck back to his cabin and Pat and I rode our horses.

We ate fresh liver that night from the renegade bull. I didn't think our adventure had been overly exciting, not really much different than our dude rides, but it was new country. We accomplished what we set out to do—we'd captured the maverick bull, although the ending was different than what we'd anticipated.

The next morning, we cinched our saddles on the side racks and prepared to leave. Pat only loaded one of his horses while I loaded both of the horses I had brought. As I tried to clean the broken windshield off the seat of the truck, I heard Pat and Mud talking.

"You take the horse," Pat was saying, "you ain't got a good one and you need a good one. And that horse is as honest as the day is long. And he's tough as nails. I've got plenty back at the ranch."

"But I ain't got the money to pay you for him," said Mud.

"I didn't ask for any money," said Pat.

"But I can't accept such an expensive horse as a gift," replied Mud.

"Well," said Pat, "let's look at it this way—I'm just lending you the horse. You need him. And you can return him to me anytime."

"Are you sure?"

"Certainly," answered Pat.

When I got the broken glass cleaned out of the truck and off the seat as best as I could, I watched the two old friends bargaining about the horse. Actually, there wasn't any bargaining, Pat wanted to give Mud the horse and Mud was reluctant to take him as a gift. It was interesting to watch, but I didn't interfere. When the matter was settled, Pat had won his case. Mud led the horse to the small pasture and Pat and I drove away.

Pat asked, "Did you get all the glass cleaned up?"

"I think so," I answered.

"You know, it was mighty uncomfortable driving this truck back to Mud's yesterday with all that glass on the seat. I even found some in my back pocket last night!"

"Better check your side of the seat now," I said, "I spent most of the time cleanin' my side of the truck."

Pat raised up in the truck and brushed the seat. He found a couple of fragments of glass. "I'm glad you told me," he said, as he brushed the glass away. "I could have punctured myself!"

There wasn't any discussion as to what we'd tell Bud about what happened; the truth would suffice. Pat knew Bud would understand about the gift of the horse to Mud.

"There's no need to explain that to Bud," said Pat. "He was one of my horses."

"How many horses do you own?"

"I've got a few," said Pat.

"I guess I'll need to take the truck to town to get a new windshield an' hood tomorrow," I said. "And we'll need to get a new rack for the front. This little venture has been kinda expensive for the ranch and you!"

"That's okay," said Pat, "I don't have anything else to spend my money on."

When we got to the ranch, we raised quite a commotion as we drove up. Everyone wanted to know what had happened. Even Bud, who had come down to the loading chute in the golf cart, was curious. Bud didn't ask any questions about the truck, but listened carefully as Pat explained the circumstances. However, he did ask, "Where's your other horse?"

"I gave him to Mud," replied Pat. "He needed him, I don't think his horse will survive, despite what Mud and Honey did for him. I'll explain later."

Pat didn't want to go into much detail about the horse being gored. What few guests were still at the ranch were present and they would understand about shooting the bull, but a horse being gored might be a little much for them.

"I'll take the truck to town tomorrow to get it fixed," I said. "I can spend the night with Sally an' Ginny an' come back with them Friday night."

Chuck asked, "If it's all right, I'd like to hitch a ride to town with you. I can catch a bus to go home."

"You want to leave this quick?" I asked.

"Yes," said Chuck. "There's been some unexpected develop-ments back home and I'm needed there."

"Whatever you want," I replied.

Quince asked, "How will you get the truck back?"

"We can leave it a week, then I can ride back with Sally on Sunday when she goes back to town so Ginny can go to school." I'd had plenty of time to figure out the details.

Before I left for town the next day, Pat came to me and said, "You have the repair bill sent to me. I'll handle it."

When I got to town, Sally met me at the repair shop. I'd called her the night before and explained the situation to her. Her greeting was simple, "What happened?"

I told her the details of the capture of the bull and the results.

"Was anybody hurt?"

"No," I answered, "just Mud's horse. Pat ended up giving Mud one of his horses."

"That's just like Pat," said Sally. "He's got a heart as big as all outdoors."

"Yep," I said, "he even said to have the repair bill on the truck sent to him."

"I'll talk to Daddy about that," said Sally.

The Makings of a Cowgirl

The next day in town was really quite boring for me and I was glad when Ginny got out of school and we could go back to the ranch. I've always been a little uncomfortable in town. Ginny could hardly wait to take a ride on the Welsh pony I'd bought for her.

"I guess you know I'll be taking out the short dude ride in the morning," said Sally. "Ginny is getting to be quite a rider for her age."

"Does that come from your side of the family or mine?" I asked.

"It might be a mixture of both sides," replied Sally.

The next morning while Sally saddled her horse, Ginny was trying to get her saddle on the pony and having a little difficulty.

Bud had come down to the corral in his wheelchair to visit and see the rides off. All the horses had gotten used to his wheelchair, so there wasn't a commotion.

Seeing Ginny having some difficulty, Bud said, "Let me help you with that, Granddaughter."

"I can get it, Grandpa," was Ginny's response.

"But your blankets aren't straight. And they're wrinkled. If you don't straighten them, your horse will get a sore back, then you won't be able to ride him." Bud rolled his wheelchair to the pony and straightened the saddle and blankets. Although he was confined to a wheelchair, he still was surprisingly strong in his upper body.

When Bud completed his straightening job, Ginny reached under the pony, grabbed the cinch, and started to tighten it. "This is the part I have a hard time with," said Ginny. "Just how tight should it be?"

"Well, Darling, it should be tight enough to keep the saddle in place, but not so tight that it will be uncomfortable for him. Here, I'll show you."

Bud tightened the cinch with the expertise of a horseman who'd saddled horses all his life. When he got done, he said, "That's about right. See how I can get a couple of fingers between the latigos and the horse? That's not too tight or too loose. Here, you slip your fingers in there and see for yourself."

Ginny did as she was told.

"Now you remember that," said Bud. "When you get bigger and have to rope something, you'll need it tighter, but that will work for now. Now untrack the horse, walk him around some, and then check the cinch again. Some horses will take a deep breath before you tighten the cinch, so you can't get it too tight. Then when you get on, the saddle will roll."

Ginny did as she was told and as she left, I walked over to Bud. He saw me coming and said, "I used to do the same thing for Sally when she was starting to ride. When Sally was first starting, she wouldn't let me tighten her cinch, and when she went to get on, the saddle rolled. That was a hard lesson for her, but she learned it well. After that, and for quite a while, she asked me to check her cinch every time she saddled up."

As Bud reminisced about Sally's upbringing, I stood there and listened.

Bud continued, "Sally was pretty headstrong when she was younger ..."

"She still is," I interrupted.

Bud laughed. "You're right! But she has gotten better over the years. Ginny is pretty headstrong, but not as much as Sally used to be. And Ginny's smart also!"

"That must come from my side of the family!" I said.

Bud laughed again. "Perhaps we can just count that up as real genetic improvement."

"Whatever," I said. "But she's a real good girl."

"You're right there," said Bud. "She reminds me a lot of Sally when she was younger."

Ginny returned. "Is this enough, Grandpa?"

"I think so. You've walked that horse around so much, he'll be so tired you won't be able to ride him very far. Check your cinch and get on. Let's see how you ride."

Ginny checked the cinch. "Is this tight enough, Grandpa?"

Bud wheeled his chair over to the horse and checked the cinch. I felt a little slighted that Ginny didn't ask me, her father, to check the cinch, but let it go. She was on great terms with her grandfather and I wanted to maintain that.

"That should be good enough," said Bud. "Now let's see you ride."

"But Mommy and Daddy aren't ready yet. I don't want to tire my horse out before we go!"

Sally approached, leading her horse, Beauty. "Go ahead and get on, Ginny, I'm ready. Honey, get your horse."

I got my old saddle horse, Roman, and joined the family. Pat, Jimmy, and Quince had saddled the dude horses for the guests.

"I checked with the guests and none of them wants to go for a short ride," said Sally. "So we can have a nice family ride, all to ourselves. Ginny, do you want to lead?"

"Sure! Follow me."

As Ginny led us out, I said to Sally, "Looks like Bud has already started Ginny's education around the horses."

"Yes," answered Sally.

"Don't you go and get us lost," I said to Ginny. "If you do, we might not make it back in time for dinner!"

"I won't get lost, I know right where we're going," asserted Ginny, as she headed out in a direction not normally used on our dude rides.

"Do you really know where you're goin', Sis?" I asked.

"Of course," answered Ginny.

"But I don't ever remember bringin' you out here before," I said. "I think you're goin' to get us lost!"

Sally didn't say anything as I tried to tease Ginny. However I think she knew where Ginny was taking us. I had a good idea, but still wanted to have some fun with Ginny.

Fairy Tales

"I've been out here a lot," said Ginny.

"When have you ever been out here?" I asked.

"Oh," said Ginny, "Grandpa has brought me out here lots of times, but always in the golf cart."

"Daddy's doing the same thing with Ginny as he did with me," said Sally, "but we always came horseback. When I was too little to ride my own horse, Pat used to hand me up to Daddy and I'd ride in front. I remember Daddy used to give me the reins and let me control the horse. I thought I was doing real well until I got older and figured out that Daddy was telling the horse where to go with his spurs. I even remember the little spotted pony Daddy got for me. I called him Dimples."

"Dimples? That sounds like something you'd name a horse," I said.

"I thought he was the best horse in the world," said Sally. "And I guess for a five- or six-year-old girl, he was. He died one winter when I was about ten or eleven. Daddy didn't tell me until I came home from boarding school. I cried for days! Daddy gave me another horse, but at the time that didn't help much. I'd almost forgotten all about it. Ginny is giving me an opportunity to relive my own childhood again. I know the best parts of it were right here on this ranch!"

I knew that where we were going was a real special spot for the Wilson family. Sally had led me up here and we'd spent our wedding night and honeymoon camped out here. It was a real pretty spot, fenced off to keep deer, elk, cattle, and horses out.

"I probably should have been bringing Ginny up here myself," said Sally. I thought Sally felt a little guilty about not bringing her daughter out here, and she showed it a little.

"Don't worry about it, Darlin'," I said. "Bud has been bringin' her out here an' keepin' up the family tradition."

"What did you and Grandpa Bud talk about when you came out here?" asked Sally.

"Grandpa would tell me funny stories about his Mommy and Daddy. Some of the stories were scary, too! And he always told me how pretty Grandma was. That's your Mommy, Mommy. I never knew her."

"I know Darling, I didn't either," said Sally, somewhat ruefully.

Sally was starting to choke up some, and seeing this, I moved my horse next to hers and put my right arm around her. She grasped my right hand and squeezed, hard.

"Easy, Darlin'," I said. Trying to lighten up the mood, I told Ginny, "Tell us some of the funny stories Grandpa told you, Sis."

"I like the one where Grandpa's daddy was in the outhouse and his horse pulled it over. He yelled and yelled and finally some of his hired hands came and put the outhouse in place again and he could get out the door."

"I remember that one," said Sally. "Daddy's father said, He 'sure wasn't going to crawl out that hole!'"

"Did your grandpa ever tell any funny stories about himself?" I asked.

"Yes," said Ginny.

I asked, "What was the funniest one?"

Ginny answered, "I think the funniest one, the one I like the best, is when he took out his false teeth, put them in his back pocket, got on his horse, sat down and bit himself in the butt!" All through the telling of this story, Ginny could hardly keep from laughing herself.

"That's one he never told me," said Sally.

"Oh! I forgot," said Ginny, "I wasn't supposed to tell anyone. You won't tell him I told, will you?"

"No, Sis," I said, "your secret is safe with us." Even as I said this, I wondered just how much fun Bud was having with his granddaughter. I think Bud stretched the truth a little to have fun with her.

"It's about time we started back," I said. "Do you want to have a race home?"

"As fast as we can go?" asked Ginny. "You know my Pumpkin is really fast. He could beat both of your horses!"

"No, Sis, a walking race. We'll see what horse can walk the fastest."

"That won't be any fun," said Ginny. "Going fast is really fun."

"Have you ever gone fast on a horse?" I asked.

"Sure," said Ginny.

"When?"

"Grandpa and I have races around in the corral all the time," answered Ginny.

"You an' Grandpa race around the corral?"

"Yep," replied Ginny. "Pumpkin and me can beat Grandpa and Dragon Slayer any time."

"I," corrected Sally.

Ginny corrected herself. "I" she said.

"Dragon Slayer? Who's that? We don't have a horse named Dragon Slayer," I said.

"Dragon Slayer is what Grandpa calls the golf cart."

"When did he start callin' the golf cart Dragon Slayer?" I asked.

"The day he killed the last fire-breathing dragon up on the top of that ridge," said Ginny, pointing to a high ridge off to the north.

I asked, "Just how did he do that?"

"Grandpa told me he was up there one day just looking around when he saw this fire-breathing dragon walking through the woods, setting the woods on fire. He didn't have a gun so he decided to run the dragon down with the golf cart. He put the dragon on the run and ran over him. He told me he had to run over him a few times just to make sure he was dead and there wouldn't be any more for-est fires. He told me that was the last fire-breathing dragon in the country, and he can prove it!"

"How can he prove it?" I asked.

"Grandpa says he's never seen another since then. And I haven't ever seen one either," said Ginny. "Have you?"

"Nope," I answered.

I could see Sally silently smiling as Ginny told her story.

As we rode toward the ranch, Sally and I held our horses back a little so Ginny could win our walking race home.

"You know," said Sally, "those are the same stories Daddy told me when I was about her age. Daddy has changed the stories to fit the times of course, but they're essentially the same. I'd forgotten all about them until today."

"You better hurry," yelled Ginny. "I'm going to beat you!"

"I'm goin' as fast as I can without breakin' into a trot," I yelled back at Ginny.

We let our horses move out a little faster, just to make our race look more like a race for Ginny's sake.

We got back to the ranch, took care of our horses, and went inside to eat. Bud and Missus Abercrombie were finishing their noon meal.

"Where did you go for your ride?" asked Bud.

"Up to our special spot," answered Sally. "Ginny tells me she's been up there a lot."

"Yes. I've taken her up there quite often, just like I used to do with you," replied Bud.

"And I understand you've named the golf cart Dragon Killer, or something like that!"

"Dragon Slayer," corrected Bud.

"Does that old golf cart have enough power to run down a fire-breathing dragon?"

"Not now," said Bud, grinning. "But that happened in its younger days and it had more power then." Bud wasn't at all embarrassed about his stretching the truth to his granddaughter and was having some fun with his daughter.

"It seems like I remember something very similar from my younger days and from the same source!" said Sally.

"You very well may have, Daughter, you very well may have!" Bud was near to laughing.

I just sat back and let this little exchange between father and daughter take place as I started to eat my noon meal. The guests that Pat, Jimmy, and Quince had taken out would be coming in soon and I wanted to be at the barn to help them and make sure everything went well.

Continuing Education

Our summer season was fast coming to an end. Each week there were fewer guests showing up. Of course school had started, so there were fewer families with kids showing up. Occasionally, we would have a family arrive with kids. When we asked them why the kids weren't in school, their reply was, "They're home-schooled."

I had never heard of "home schooling," so I asked Sally about it.

"It's something new, where parents can keep their kids home and do their education themselves."

"How's it workin'?"

"I don't know," answered Sally. "But the youngsters are supposed to get a degree when they're done. Don't you remember that I looked into it for Ginny, but we decided it would be better for Ginny to go to a public school and make friends and learn to get along with others."

I thought about it and decided that some of the lessons I'd learned at home were more valuable and educational than what I had learned in school.

I planned for the upcoming activities for the fall. We had to gather cattle, sort off the calves, and prepare for our cattle sale. Before we had the sale, we'd need to pregnancy check all the cows. We'd have to select some replacement heifers and cull some older cows, open cows, and bulls. We'd need to go to some bull sales and buy a few bulls to replace those that we culled.

We'd also need to prepare for our annual registered paint horse sale. Bud had indicated that we probably ought to slim down our broodmare bunch and just run one stud bunch rather than two, as we had before our main stud was shot by Dusty Waters.

We would provide a place to stay for our cow and horse buyers and meals for them. We'd charge those individuals that didn't buy anything. We'd learned from past experience that some of our supposed customers just came out to get a free weekend of room and board. Those individuals that bought something wouldn't be charged anything. This discouraged some buyers that weren't serious about buying and consequently fewer buyers showed up. That was fine, because we only wanted serious buyers.

I thought we would probably need to run in our stud bunch and decide what to sell and what to keep. When we had made those decisions, Sally could take pictures of the mares we wanted to sell and include them in a sale catalog. We'd need to decide what green broke colts to sell and include them in the catalog.

There was plenty to do and I was thankful we didn't take in hunters for the deer and elk season. Thinking about the upcoming hunting seasons, I remembered that we'd have to go around the perimeters of the ranch and repost the "NO HUNTING" signs. A lot of the hunters didn't know that the white paint on the top of the steel posts on the fence indicated that the property was posted. As we did this, we could check the fence and make minor repairs. The major repairs we would make in the spring, after the snow was gone. Sometimes the snowdrifts would weigh the fence down. If we had any guests, and they were up to it, they could accompany us on these longer rides.

There was plenty to do, and I took a pencil and pocket-sized notebook from my pocket and made a note—pick up NO HUNTING signs. Sally could pick up the signs in town.

We'd had our hay delivered periodically during the summer by Bud's brother, Fred. I was glad this was already done, one less thing to worry about. We had more than enough to get the cattle and horses through the winter. Thinking about Fred, I thought of Bud's other brother, what was his name? I could see in my mind's eye his face as clear as day, but couldn't recall his name. All of the sudden, it came to me—Rod! That was it. I hadn't seen Rod for a year or two and wondered how he was doing. He was an old bachelor and ran a sizeable sheep herd farther to the west. He didn't have a car or truck, he did all his traveling horseback. When he needed to go to town, he'd go to Fred's and one of Fred's hands would drive him.

It looked like we'd stay pretty busy during the fall. I decided I'd ask the woman from town if she could stay until after our cattle and horse sales to help close up the cabins. Sally and Missus Abercrombie couldn't do it all on the weekends, and if Missus Abercrombie stayed, she'd try to do it alone.

I started making notes about all that we'd have to do to get ready for fall, there was enough that I was afraid I wouldn't remember it all.

I enjoyed this time of year. The nights were cool, some of them downright cold. But the days were generally nice and warm. It was Indian summer and the leaves on the aspens and oak brush were turning color. I kinda felt sorry for the guests that had to leave or had already left. The dudes always made comments about how pretty it was out here, but most of them missed the fall colors, the best time of the year.

I decided we should gather the broodmare bunch and run them in one Friday. Then on Saturday, when Sally was here, she, Bud, Pat, and I could make the decisions as to what mares to keep and what mares to sell. Quince had already left to return to school, but Jimmy was still here. He would be a lot of help.

That was the plan and Sally was disappointed she wouldn't be able to help run the horses in. But she saw the sensibility in the idea and agreed. She really liked running the horses, it was fast and quite often exciting. She always helped when we brought in the saddle horses, usually at a run.

The Friday we had chosen to run in the horses arrived. Early in the morning, Pat, Jimmy, and I saddled our best horses and set out to find the stud bunch. After a couple of hours of riding, we located the broodmares. We'd gone through a couple of pastures and left the gates open. A rough count indicated all the broodmares were there. The new stud was doing a good job of controlling his mares.

I told Pat, "Jimmy an' I can lead 'em in if you want to follow."

"I always get the dust-eating job," said Pat, jokingly.

"I can follow, if you want to lead," I said.

"No, that's all right," said Pat. "You know the way, don't you?"

It was my turn to laugh. "I think so. Don't worry about closin' any of the gates, we'll be bringin' 'em back this way."

Pat gave me a knowing nod. I kinda felt foolish as he didn't need to be told that.

"Well," said Jimmy, "it looks like I'm the only leader here as I haven't even been considered to follow!"

Pat and I both laughed and we started out, Jimmy and I taking the lead and Pat following the bunch. I was glad to have Pat following the mares. I knew he wouldn't push them too fast and have them pass Jimmy and me. The mares followed and we maintained a brisk trot until we reached the first gate. We slowed down as we didn't want to have a wreck and get any of the mares tangled in the fence.

Leading the mares in wasn't hard, we just had to make sure none of the mares wanted to veer off in a different direction. Pat had it pretty easy, he just followed. The stud actually drove the horses and kept up the stragglers. We put the broodmare bunch in the little pasture where we'd kept the orphaned colt and another mare and colt. They'd be easy to corral in the morning and there was enough feed to keep them overnight.

Bud watched from the main corral as we brought the horses in. "They look good, don't they!"

The cook and Missus Abercrombie were with him. They agreed.

Pat, Jimmy, and I took care of our horses and turned them loose for the night. We kept in four other horses to use in the morning to corral the broodmares. The fourth horse would be for Sally to ride. We probably could have corralled them on foot, but this was a ranch and cowboys don't do anything on foot if they can help it.

It was after dark when Sally and Ginny arrived. They were excited about seeing the horses, but couldn't until the next morning.

At supper, Bud outlined the plan for the next day. Sally would take pictures of the mares we decided to sell. Pat and I would rope the mares that were hard to catch. Jimmy would halter the mares, they'd all been halter broken as younger horses, and lead them to where Bud and Sally could evaluate them. Sally had all their registration papers, but could identify most of them from memory. The registration papers had the year they were born so we could use that to determine their exact age. Pat or I would mouth the horses to see what kind of shape their teeth were in. Pat and I could voice our opinions as we felt necessary. When a decision was made as to whether to keep or sell a particular mare, Jimmy would turn them loose in either a keeper pen or a sale pen. We'd try to bring the colts with the mares, so we could keep them together. Having the colts present would be helpful in making the determination whether to keep or sell. We could see what kind of colts the mares raised.

With the plan established, we all went to bed. It looked like it was going to be a long day tomorrow.

The next morning, I was surprised that Ginny was up early.

"What gets you up so early, Sis?" I asked.

"Grandpa said I could pick a colt to be my very own today. I wanted to get up early and pick out a good one. Someday, I'll be too big to ride Pumpkin. And when the colt gets big enough, I'll break him myself!"

"All by yourself?"

"Grandpa told me he'd help me if I needed it. But he didn't think I'd need it."

"We forgot to keep Pumpkin in last night, so you wait here with Grandpa and Missus Abercrombie, then come down to the corrals with Grandpa," I said. "You can look at all the colts then, okay?"

Ginny looked disappointed because she couldn't look at the colts right away, but she had been well instructed to do what she was told when we were working livestock.

Pat and Jimmy were already saddling their horses when Sally and I arrived at the barn.

"Decided to sleep in a little this morning?" Pat asked, grinning.

Sally just smiled and caught her horse and started brushing him. She was used to this kind of good-natured kidding from Pat.

"Yep," I answered, "I decided a few extra winks wouldn't hurt me."

"If you were looking to get some beauty rest," said Jimmy, "it didn't take!"

We all laughed.

"Is my horse saddled yet?" I asked.

"No," said Pat. "We weren't sure you were comin' or not, so we decided to wait." I caught up my horse and started brushing him. "I'm sure I can saddle him, in spite of your snide remarks."

Soon I had my horse saddled and we were headed for the small pasture to bring in the broodmares. The good-natured ribbing and kidding went on every morning, with all the hands, although with the new hands at the beginning of the summer season it took them awhile to get used to it. I figured it added to the relaxed but efficient work atmosphere and actually looked forward to it each day.

The mares weren't hard to run in and we had the job done quickly. Pat caught the young stud and tied him in a corral adjacent to the big corral the mares were in.

"Before we do anything else, I think we need to go to the house an' get some breakfast," I said.

Nobody argued and we all went to the lodge. Bud, Ginny, Missus Abercrombie, the cook, and the woman I hired to help out, were waiting for us. They were just finishing their breakfast.

"I'm ready to go get my colt, Daddy," said Ginny.

"You'll need to wait until we eat," I said.

Ginny looked disappointed.

"And you'll need a coat!" said Sally. "Go to your room and get one. It's cold out there this morning.

The little girl obediently did as she was told.

"I don't know why she's so anxious this morning," said Sally.

"I know why," I said. "Grandpa Bud told her she could pick out a colt for herself this morning. She's excited."

Bud beamed. "Yep," he said. "Ginny is just as excited as you were when you got to pick out a horse to replace your first pony. What was his name, Puddles? Poodles? Something like that."

"Dimples," replied Sally. "We were just talking about that the other day."

Ginny returned with her coat already on and started toward the door.

"You need to wait for us, Sis," I said. "We'll be ready shortly, as soon as we finish eatin'."

Rachel, the woman I'd hired asked, "Can I come down and look at the horses?"

"Certainly, Rachel," replied Sally. "You've never been on a ride with us, you can go anytime you want!"

"Oh, I'm not a rider," said Rachel, "I'm actually scared of them, they're so big! But I do like to watch them, they're so beautiful!"

"Well, you can come down and watch all day if you want," said Sally.

After breakfast, we all went down to the corral, with Ginny leading. She headed right for the gate and started to open it.

"Hold on there, Sis!" I shouted. "Don't go in there unless I'm with you or Mommy."

"Hurry up!" was Ginny's response.

Bud laughed. "She's just like her mom when she was that age!"

"Jimmy, go to the barn an' bring back a couple or three halters," I said. "We'll try to catch these horses on foot before we have to start ropin' 'em. It might be kinda tough, a lot of these mares haven't been handled for a few years."

When Jimmy returned with the halters, I told Ginny, "You sit on the fence, outside with Grandpa. You can look at each one of the colts as we catch their moms. Rachel, I'd appreciate it if you'd help Bud and Missus Abercrombie keep an eye on Ginny. She's pretty fast."

I knew Ginny could get into the corral faster than either Bud or Missus Abercrombie could stop her and I didn't want to run the risk of her getting in the corral and getting run over by the horses.

"I'd be glad to watch her, Mister Honey," said Rachel.

Rachel had always called me "Mister Honey."

"You can drop the Mister," I said. I'd told her that before, but it didn't do any good. I doubted if it would this time either.

Carrying halters, Jimmy, Pat, and I entered the corral. Although all the mares had been halter broke, seeing a man on foot made them a little uneasy and they milled around the corral nervously, stirring up a lot of dust.

Jimmy finally cornered a mare and Pat and I helped get her haltered. Jimmy led the mare over to where Sally was standing by the fence. Bud was outside the corral in his wheelchair.

Before Sally could call out the name of the mare, Bud said, "She's a keeper!"

Ignoring Bud, Pat mouthed the horse. "Her teeth are all right, although she's missing a tooth. I'd judge her to be about ten," he said.

"Eleven," corrected Sally. She'd found the mare's registration papers and looked at the birth date.

"She's got a lot of years left," said Bud. "And she always has good spotted colts! Put her in the keeper pen! Do you like her colt, Ginny?"

"I like all of them!" replied Ginny.

The morning went much like that. We'd catch a mare, identify her, mouth her, and look at her colt. A few older mares were put in the sale pen, but most of the mares went to the keeper pen. After a while, Pat and I got our saddle horses and started to rope the mares that were harder to catch. Most of the mares we roped stopped trying to get away when they felt the rope around their necks, they'd been halter broke as young colts and remembered their learning.

Ginny was given the opportunity to look at each colt as the mothers were being mouthed, but couldn't make up her mind. She still hadn't picked one and the number of choices was dwindling.

The saddle horses, not being driven to the corrals that morning, showed up at the corrals looking for their grain. I opened the gate and they went into a separate corral. *They'll keep right there until we need to pick a couple of fresh horses to take the broodmare bunch back to their pasture,* I thought.

Sally and I hadn't noticed, but Ginny had moved to the far side of the corral. Rachel and Missus Abercrombie were with her and she was all right. But she had her arm through the fence and was petting a colt.

"I want this one!" she shouted.

From where he was seated, Bud couldn't see the colt Ginny had picked. I looked up from what I was doing and saw Ginny petting the colt. Jimmy smiled and said, "Why that's the orphaned colt I've been taking care of. He's already halter broke and he follows me around like a puppy dog."

Bud wheeled his chair around to where Ginny was.

"That's the one you want?"

"Yep," said Ginny. "I like him and he likes me! See?" Ginny continued to pet the colt.

Jimmy got one of the halters Pat and I had been using and came over and haltered the colt. He took the colt outside the corral and handed the lead rope to Ginny.

"Here," he said, "you lead him around and see if he likes you good enough to follow you."

"Are you sure that's okay?" asked Sally.

"That colt is as gentle as anything on the ranch," answered Jimmy. "I've spent a lot of time with him, teaching him manners ever since you brought him here. Nothing seems to spook him and he acts like he's got some sense. He's a fast learner."

Much to the dismay of Sally, Ginny took the rope and led the colt around. The colt followed nicely and Sally relaxed. Jimmy had done a good job of halter breaking and gentling the colt.

"What are you going to name him?" asked Missus Abercrombie.

"I don't know yet," answered Ginny.

"Seeing as that's your horse now, we'll have to give him extra care and attention," said Bud.

"He's been getting extra care and attention ever since he got here," said Jimmy. "I've been giving it to him every day!"

Bud smiled. "I guess you're right," he said.

"Now that Ginny's colt has been selected, let's get back to work," I said. "Jimmy, tie that colt up and Ginny, you look at the other colts. You might see one you like better."

"But I like this one, Daddy!"

"Okay," I said.

"Jimmy, come over here," said Bud.

When Jimmy went to Bud, Bud said, "I was going to give you that colt because you've spent a lot of extra time with him. But now, my granddaughter wants him and …"

"I understand," interrupted Jimmy.

"I was going to say, before I was so rudely interrupted, that because of the situation, I will give you your pick of any of the horses on the ranch, as long as their mine. You can't pick one of Honey's, or Pat's, or Sally's."

"You don't have to do that, Bud," said Jimmy.

"I know, but I want to. I was going to give you the colt because I thought being orphaned as he was, he'd be stunted and perhaps a slow learner. But if he is stunted, he'll still be the right size for Ginny when she gets bigger. So you go ahead and pick a horse you want."

"Well," said Jimmy, "I do kinda like the horse I've been riding, Digger."

"That's done then. Digger is yours. Consider it an early Christmas gift or bonus."

"But I don't have a place to keep him at school," said Jimmy.

"He'll be just fine here," said Bud.

"Thanks, Bud. And even if it is early, Merry Christmas!"

Jimmy left smiling and Bud was smiling, too.

Sally and I had heard the conversation and Sally smiled. "That's Daddy. I swear he'd give away the whole ranch if he thought it would make someone smile."

"They don't come any finer," I said.

We hadn't noticed, but Ginny had disappeared. A frantic visual search of the corral showed that she wasn't there. Her colt was tied to the fence.

"Where could she have gone?" questioned Missus Abercrombie.

"She was here just a minute ago," said Rachel, "she can't be far off."

"Here she comes," said Jimmy.

Ginny was coming from the barn, dragging her saddle and a horse blanket.

Sally rushed to her. "Where have you been? You know you're not supposed to leave us when we're working livestock!"

"I didn't leave," said Ginny. "I just went to the barn."

"What for?" asked Sally.

"To get my saddle," answered Ginny. "I've got it right here, see!"

"And what do you think you're going to do with it?" asked Sally.

Bud was clearly amused by the situation, once the seriousness of a missing little girl was dismissed, and started to laugh.

Ginny answered, "I've picked my horse and now I'm going to start breaking him!"

"Oh really!" Sally sounded both amused and somewhat bewildered.

"My colt isn't as big as Pumpkin. I'll bet I can get the saddle on him and keep the blankets straight, like Grandpa says. I don't want him to get a sore back."

"I should give you a good spanking for leaving us like that. You had us all scared to death!" said Sally.

"Now, now, Daughter," said Bud, coming to the little girl's defense. "Don't be too hasty. I didn't always give you a spanking when I thought you needed it! Or deserved it!"

"But," said Sally, "I do seem to remember some I did get that I didn't think I needed, deserved, or earned!"

"That might be true," said Bud, smiling, "but Ginny's just excited about picking out her own horse."

Jimmy came over. "Let me take your saddle and blanket. I haven't had a saddle on him and he might fight it a little."

"But I want to break him myself," said Ginny.

"Oh, you'll break him yourself," said Jimmy. "I'm just helping out a little. You better brush him before you saddle him."

This seemed to suit Ginny and she started to go to the barn to get a brush.

"Just where do you think you're going, little girl?" Sally sounded quite upset and perturbed, just like my mother sounded with me when I was younger and had done something wrong. I decided that all mothers sounded alike when they were upset.

"I'm just going to the barn to get a brush," answered Ginny.

In the same tone of voice all mothers use when upset, Sally told her daughter, "You need to tell me where you're going before you leave and report back to me when you get back!"

"Yes, Mommy!" Ginny's answer was so sweet and innocent, Sally lost the sternness she had been using.

As Ginny headed toward the barn, Sally turned to me and said, "Honey, I think we're going to have our hands full with her from here on out."

"What do you mean?" I asked.

Sally gave me a quizzical look.

"My hands have been full ever since I married you!"

Everyone except Sally laughed. She just smiled.

Ginny returned with a brush.

Jimmy said, "Go brush your colt. Do a good job and be sure to brush under his belly, where the cinch goes, really good. We don't want him to get a cinch sore."

Ginny went to the colt and started brushing him.

"Jimmy," asked Sally, "just how do you propose to saddle the horse without getting Ginny hurt?"

"You'll see. Right now, just brushing the horse will keep her occupied. If you, Honey, and Pat can finish up without me, I'll keep an eye on her."

Having watched the whole situation develop and become resolved satisfactorily, I said, "We can finish up. Just remember, Jimmy, babysittin' don't pay any more than regular wages!"

Everyone laughed and we returned to our work. Sally kept glancing nervously in Jimmy and Ginny's direction, but everything was all right over there. Ginny was brushing the colt and Jimmy was standing by the colt's head where he could control the colt just in case something went wrong.

Presently, Jimmy said, "I think you've got him pretty well brushed." Picking up the small blanket and saddle, Jimmy started toward the colt.

The colt hadn't seen a saddle before and as Jimmy approached, the colt stepped backward.

"Look at that," said Jimmy. "This colt has never seen a blanket and saddle before and it scares him a little. We don't want him to be scared of that, do we?"

"No," said Ginny.

"Then I'll tell you what I think we ought to do."

"What's that?" asked Ginny.

"I think we ought to set this saddle and blanket right here on the ground in front of him and let your colt get used to it. When he finds out it won't bite him or otherwise hurt him, he'll let us put it on him. Does that sound good to you?"

"Yes," said Ginny. "We don't want to scare him."

Jimmy dropped the saddle and blanket on the ground and the colt tried to take another step backward.

"He'll get used to that," said Jimmy. "It's better if he can learn this lesson on his own. Let's go see if we can help your mom and dad."

Ginny agreed and soon they were both seated on the top rail of the fence, watching.

I noticed them on the fence and said, "Jimmy, if you want to help out here, I'll watch my daughter."

"I can do that, Honey," said Jimmy. "Just remember, babysitting doesn't pay any more than regular wages!"

Everyone laughed and Jimmy got his horse. I rode over to where Ginny was sitting on the fence and put her in front of me. She could ride around with me while everyone else finished up.

"Let's count the horses Grandpa Bud has decided to cull," I said. "Can you count?"

"Sure," said Ginny, and she proceeded to prove it by counting. "One, two, three, four."

I stopped her. "Save it for when we're counting the horses." I could see her counting to a hundred without stopping. We started when we got alongside the sale pen. "Now you can start."

Ginny continued, "Five, six, seven, eight."

"Wait a minute! Start with one! You'll end up having too many horses in this pen. We'll count them together."

We counted them twice before we could agree on the number—

twelve. Bud was culling the broodmare bunch a little lighter than I had expected him to. If my figures were right, that would leave the young stud with twenty-six mares to handle. I thought that might be a few too many for him.

When they got done, Bud had ended up putting thirteen in the sale pen. "Do you think he can control twenty-five mares?" I asked Bud.

"He can do it," replied Bud.

Contented that he had culled sufficiently, Bud told Sally to get the camera. "Take good pictures of each mare we're selling and take a lot!" he said. "We'll use the best ones in the sale catalog. Pat, you and Honey and Jimmy probably ought to run in those yearling colts you halter broke last winter. We'll get pictures of them and maybe pair up some with their mothers and sell them as a package deal. Honey, those two-year-old colts you've been riding, how many of them are ready for the sale?"

"They've all been ridden quite a bit an' they're all ready," I said.

"You pick out what we want to keep and we'll get pictures of all of them we want to sell. I hope Sally brought enough film. Let's run them in and get the pictures."

"They're already in," I said.

Bud looked surprised. He hadn't seen the saddle horses come in, he'd been preoccupied picking out the sale mares.

"The saddle horses came in all by themselves an' I closed the gate behind 'em," I said.

I put Ginny on the ground, tied up my horse, and Jimmy and I went to get more halters. If we had all the two-year-olds caught and tied to the corral fence, Sally could get her pictures faster and while she was photographing them we could run in the yearling colts, they weren't far away.

Before we started to run in the yearlings, Bud decided it was dinnertime. Actually, it was past dinnertime, it was one thirty. We'd been so busy, we hadn't noticed the time.

Pat said, "You go to the house. I'll be up after I give the stud a drink."

I'd been busy enough that I'd forgotten the young stud was

tied in an adjoining pen. Pat hadn't forgot and, once again, I really appreciated the fact that he worked here. He did a nice job of covering up some of my oversights. I'd thanked him previously for similar actions, but he'd just say, "It's just part of the job."

When we went to the lodge to eat, Bud asked the cook, "Why didn't you call us for the noon meal?"

The cook answered, "I knew you were busy and didn't want to bother you. What I have for you to eat is just cold cuts and leftovers. They'll keep until you're ready."

"We're ready now," said Bud.

"So am I," said the cook.

Sally hadn't returned to the corrals. She was seated at the table eating her noon meal. "Better get some now," she said. "I've was so hungry, I'm afraid I haven't left much for you!"

"There's plenty," said the cook, setting another plate of cold cuts on the table.

"Honey," said Sally, "you take Ginny and wash her hands. Look at her, she's filthy! Wash her face, too! And while you're at it, you wash up!"

"We all better wash," said Bud.

After we cleaned up, we sat down and ate heartily.

While she had been eating, Sally had been thinking. She told Bud, "I have some pictures of the boys using the two-year-old colts when we were branding and gathering cattle. Missus Abercrombie took a lot of them. Why don't we include some of them in our catalog? We'd be showing the colts in their working clothes. Besides that, I get tired of looking at all the sale catalogs with the horses posed and brushed so perfectly."

"That's a good idea," said Bud, "we'll do it. Those pictures of the horses being used don't have to be perfect. Just don't select any of Blake getting bucked off when he broke his wrist!"

We all laughed. Pictures of a bucking horse in a saddle horse and broodmare catalog weren't appropriate.

"That colt that bucked Blake off, you've been riding him Honey. How's he coming along?"

"He's doin' just fine," I said. "He hasn't even offered to do anything other than what he's been asked to do. He's given me a hundred percent all the time. When he bucked Blake off, I think it was a fluke an' Blake could have stopped him, but I think he wanted to show off a little."

"He showed us what he can't do!" said Bud.

We all laughed. It was really the first time we'd actually laughed at Blake's misfortune.

After dinner, Pat, Jimmy, and I caught the two-year-olds, tied them to the fence, and then went to gather the yearlings. A lot of them came out to meet us as we approached. They'd been pretty much left alone during the summer and were curious as to the approaching horses.

"Jimmy," I said, "you lead this little bunch of horses in. Pat an' I will follow. Take 'em at a pretty fast trot, they're young yet an' might want to play on the way. Don't let any get ahead of you. You lead 'em right in the corral an' stay in there with 'em until Pat or I closes the gate."

"Okay," said Jimmy, "but how will I get out?"

Pat and I both laughed. We knew Jimmy was joking.

"We'll let you out if you do a good job," said Pat.

Still laughing, I said, "Before you start, let's make a little circle around this pasture just to make sure we got 'em all. I'm not sure how many we turned in here last spring. When you see us comin' you can start."

Pat and I made a short ride around the pasture, found four more colts and started them toward Jimmy and the other yearlings.

Jimmy started and the yearlings followed. Some of the colts wanted to pass Jimmy, but he kept them behind him until he reached the corral.

Sally had pretty well got all her pictures when we arrived with the yearlings. I let Jimmy out of the corral and jokingly, he said, "Thanks! I was concerned about that!" I laughed and closed the gate behind him.

We started to catch the colts and tie them to the fence. Because they were curious and had been halter broke as weaner colts, we caught most of them without having to rope many. In fact, we only had to rope two and we were careful not to let them hit the end of the rope hard. I was concerned that they might not remember their earlier training as well as the older horses. Repetition was a big part of a young horse's training because young horses tend to forget quite easily.

Sally took pictures of each one of the colts. Contented that she had enough pictures of each one, she said, "I'm done and have about run out of film. You guys can take the yearlings back and turn them loose."

I said, "I'm thinkin' that maybe we ought to take the sale mares an' their colts back together. It'll save a day gatherin' the broodmare bunch again an' sortin' 'em. They should mix well an' maybe the older mares can teach the yearlin's some manners."

Bud had been listening. "That's a good idea, Honey. Do it! I knew we kept you around here for a reason!"

I laughed and said, "I figured I would. Jimmy, you an' Sally take the lead. Pat an' I will follow. We left the gates open. We'll let the mares an' their colts follow you, then bring the yearlings on their heels. Take 'em a good way into their pasture, then circle back. Don't bring 'em back with you!"

Jimmy and Sally started and it wasn't long before we had that little bunch of mares, colts, and yearlings where we wanted them. I closed the gate when Jimmy and Sally returned then we started for home.

On the way back, Sally and I rode together. Sally expressed some concern about Ginny. "She's becoming very independent," said Sally. "Someone will have to watch her constantly when we're out here on the weekends. Did you see the way she just walked off to get her saddle and never said anything? She …"

"She's probably just like her mother was when her mother was that age," I interrupted.

"Oh, Honey, I was a perfect child! I never even thought of doing what she did without checking with Daddy."

"Dare we ask Bud about that?" I asked.

"Certainly," replied Sally, "he'll tell you I was a model child."

"I'll make it a point to ask him," I said.

Sally's Early Years

When we got back to the ranch, Ginny had convinced Rachel that it was okay to pet her colt "as long as she was present." Rachel, not having overcome her fear of horses, had kept her distance until Missus Abercrombie consented to stand close by. Rachel was petting the colt on the head, somewhat tentatively. Bud was close by, but not too close. He didn't want his wheelchair to spook the colt.

"Everything okay here?" I asked, as I rode up

"We're okay," said Ginny. "I'm letting Rachel pet my horse!"

Missus Abercrombie gave a nod of approval. I turned to Bud and said, "Bud, at supper I need to talk to you."

"Oh?" answered Bud. "Serious?"

"Not really," I answered. "But I've some questions to ask you about Sally. I think she's tryin' to mislead me."

"Supper will be fine then," said Bud, grinning.

"We'll put the stud bunch in the small pasture for the night an' take 'em back to their range in the mornin'."

"That'll be fine," said Bud. "What are you going to do with Ginny's colt?"

I hadn't given Ginny's colt any thought. "I guess we'll keep him in the small pen, next to our jingle horses.

"Will he be alone?" asked Ginny.

"Well, no," I said. "He'll be in the pen right next to where I'm puttin' my horse."

Ginny started to look a little disappointed, so I quickly added, "It'll be just like he has his own bedroom!"

That seemed to brighten her spirits. To get the stud bunch to the little pasture where they were going to spend the night, all we had to do was open a gate. They could go down the lane to the pasture and find feed and water.

Pat had opened the gate and was letting the horses out. When they left the corral, he untied the stud, took off the halter, and turned him loose. He didn't waste any time getting to his mares.

Sally and Jimmy had already unsaddled their horses and Pat and I passed them returning to where Ginny, Bud, Missus Abercrombie, and Rachel were as we took our horses to the barn to unsaddle them.

"We'll put Ginny's colt in the pen next to where we keep the jingle horses," I told Sally as we passed. She nodded knowingly and continued on.

Sally went right to Ginny and said, "We need to put him up for the night. Let's see if we can lead him to his corral."

Sally took the colt's lead rope and started toward the barn.

"I can do that!" cried Ginny, reaching for the lead rope Sally was holding.

"Wait a minute," said Jimmy. "Who's going to take this saddle and blanket back?"

"Oh!" said Ginny, handing the lead rope back to her mother. "I guess I'll have to."

"I have an idea, if you'll let me," said Jimmy.

"What's that?" asked Sally.

"Well," said Jimmy, "the saddle is going to be carried by the colt when he gets bigger. Why don't you let me saddle him and let him carry the saddle to the barn? Will you let me do that, Ginny?"

"I guess so," said Ginny, somewhat apprehensive. "But I'm going to break him to ride myself!"

"You sure are," replied Jimmy. "Now, you better stand back. He's never been saddled before and he might get scared and try to run off. I'd hate for him to run over his new owner."

Sally said, "Come stand by me and we'll help Jimmy if he needs it."

Ginny obediently stood next to her mother, holding her hand.

Jimmy took the blanket, rubbed it over the colt a little, put it in place, and picked up the saddle. He talked to both the colt and Ginny as he placed the saddle on the colt's back.

"I knew," he said, "just looking at this saddle would help him some. Look there, Ginny, he's almost broke now!"

Jimmy wiggled the saddle on the colt's back, taking his time. Presently, he reached under the horse's belly and grabbed the cinch. "We need to go real easy here so we don't get him cinch bound," said Jimmy. His comments were directed toward Ginny, but they also had a calming effect on the colt.

As Jimmy drew the cinch, the colt did kick.

"Did he kick at you, Jimmy?" asked Ginny.

"No, he was just kicking at a fly."

Jimmy slowly tightened the cinch with no further resistance from the colt.

"We'll just let him stand there for a little bit to get used to this new development. Then we'll lead him to the barn and unsaddle him. Do you think he's doing okay, Ginny?"

"Yes," answered Ginny. "Can I ride him to the barn?"

"We better wait a little before you start riding him. He needs to get used to this saddle first. And you're too big to ride him. Remember, he's just a baby!"

"I forgot," said Ginny. "Look Daddy, my colt's almost broke."

Pat and I had returned from turning our horses loose.

"It sure looks like it. Did you do it?"

"Yes," replied Ginny. "I let Jimmy help, though."

Jimmy smiled and I could see he was having a hard time not laughing out loud.

"Let's see if this little guy will lead with a saddle on," said Jimmy, as he took a few steps in a circle. The colt followed, although haltingly at first. After a few small circles, the colt relaxed and Jimmy started toward the barn.

"Ginny," hollered Jimmy, "why don't you come up here and help me just in case this guy gives me some problems?"

We had all followed as Jimmy and the colt started toward the barn, except Bud. He headed toward the lodge.

When Jimmy called for Ginny, she started to run toward him and the colt jumped forward and turned to see what was running behind him. Ginny was excited about doing everything with her colt, although Jimmy was actually doing it.

As Ginny started to run forward and the colt jumped sideways, I said, in a very stern voice, "Just walk, Sis! Just walk!"

Sally looked at me in surprise. I'd never used a stern voice around her before. Ginny slowed down to a very slow walk.

Jimmy had stopped and had reassured the colt. As Ginny approached, he said, "You better walk up here so this little guy knows you weren't running after him to hurt him. Pet him on the neck a little bit so he knows everything is okay."

Ginny did as instructed and soon the colt was acting like nothing had happened. Everyone continued toward the barn.

Upon reaching the barn, Jimmy said, "I better take off the saddle. The flies are worse in here than they are outside. Ginny, you'll have to put it on the rack."

"Okay," said Ginny, as Jimmy handed her the small kid's saddle. Ginny got it on the rack and turned around just as Jimmy tossed the blanket to her.

"Here!" Jimmy's one word was the only warning she got and the blanket hit her in the chest. She didn't know whether to laugh or cry. When she saw everyone laughing, she decided to laugh also.

Feeling a little embarrassed that he'd hit the bosses' daughter directly, Jimmy said, "You're a horse trainer now. You have to learn to take the good with the bad. Let's put this colt in his pen. I'll bring a bale of hay over and you can feed him. There's a water trough in the corral, make sure it's full."

They turned the colt loose. Jimmy brought a bale of hay over and broke it open. While Ginny was filling the water trough, Jimmy came to me and apologized for tossing the blanket at Ginny.

"That's not necessary," I said. "It was just done in fun. And Ginny might realize that she's becoming one of the hands and not 'the bosses daughter.' There's no harm done. Where did you learn how to handle kids like that?"

"School," answered Jimmy. "I had a few classes about child psychology and even one dealing with juvenile delinquents."

"Are you saying my child is a juvenile delinquent?" I asked, rather adamantly.

Jimmy laughed, "No, she's far from being that. But I did learn something about getting youngsters to do something they don't want to do. It's kinda sneaky, but I thought I'd try it on Ginny. It appears to work."

Quietly, I was very proud of my young daughter.

After we had caught up the horses we wanted to use the next day, we fed them and turned the other horses loose. We decided to call it a day and went to the house for supper.

While we were eating, Bud asked me, "What was it you wanted to talk to me about, Honey? Can we talk about it in front of everybody?"

"Sure," I said. "It seems that Sally is trying to convince me she was a perfect child when she was younger. Is this true?"

Bud laughed. "She was far from perfect, but all in all, she was pretty good."

"She's tryin' to make me believe that she never went off like Ginny did, without tellin' anybody. Is that true?"

Bud laughed again. "No. She was always slipping away to do something or explore something. The funniest thing she did, is it all right to tell this, Sally?"

"I'm sure it is, as it will probably be a figment of your imagination," replied Sally.

Again, Bud laughed. "Well, Sally was about Ginny's age, maybe a little older. Pat and I and a few other hands we had working with us were doing something at the old corrals where we brand now. This was before we started taking in dudes ... er, guests. Sally had come along riding her spotted pony, Pimples or Puddles or something like that. Well ..."

"Dimples," Sally corrected.

"Yes," said Bud, "Dimples. I never could get his name right and it's been a long time. Anyway, we were busy working and didn't see Sally anywhere. When we took a break we didn't see Sally or her pony. I immediately became concerned and we got our horses and went to look for her. Before we left, we split up. I sent everyone in a different direction to hunt for her. After we left, about a mile away, Pat spotted Dimples slowly walking back to the corrals without Sally. He caught the pony and backtracked the pony to where he had come from. He finally came across Sally, in a small beaver pond. She was swimming."

Pat laughed. "I remember that," he said.

"You finish the story, Pat. You were the one that found Sally," said Bud.

Laughing, Pat continued the story. "Well. I saw Sally swimmin', butt naked, in that beaver pond, so I hollered, 'What are you doing?' Sally's reply was, 'Swimming.' 'How come?' I asked. Sally said, 'I was hot and dirty, so I thought I'd cool off and get cleaned up.' I told her, 'You get out of that pool and come with me!' She said, 'I can't.' When I asked, 'How come?' she said, 'I don't have any clothes on and I don't have a towel.' I said, 'Put your clothes on wet. You're going to get sunburned goin' back like that.' She said, 'Okay, but don't look.' I turned around and she got dressed and came to where I was holding her horse. I told her, 'Your Pa is worried sick. You didn't tell him where you were goin'!' She said, 'I know. I was afraid if I told him, he wouldn't let me go!' We met Bud on the way back and Sally had to tell her story all over again." Pat finished his story, laughing hard.

Bud was having a good laugh also. "I'd almost forgotten about that," he said, when he stopped laughing.

Sally was smiling, just a little embarrassed. "Perhaps I was a little headstrong," she admitted.

"A little!" exclaimed Bud. "What about the time you roped a cow that didn't need roping and you didn't get your dallies? That cow dragged you off your horse and started to drag you through the sagebrush. Pat and I had to rope that cow just to get your rope off. When I asked you, 'How come you didn't let go,' you simply said, 'I didn't want to lose her.' When I asked you, 'Why did you rope her in the first place?' your reply was, 'I wanted to see if I could catch her.' If I remember right, you almost caught a good licking from me."

I was enjoying hearing about the earlier years. I hadn't heard much about them in the past.

"What about the time you were thinking about selling the ranch?" asked Missus Abercrombie. "You had some prospective buyers out here and they asked if you had many rattlesnakes."

"Ah … yes," replied Bud, reflecting on the past. "Those were some pretty tough years, before we started taking in dudes. When the prospective buyers asked if we had many rattlesnakes here, I answered, not wanting to lie to them, 'Oh, we've got our share, I imagine.' Sally heard the question and went to the office and brought a shoebox full of rattles we'd cut off the snakes we'd killed that summer. She showed the box to the buyers and said, 'These are from the snakes we've killed this year.' Needless to say, the buyers left and we never saw them again. I was pretty upset with Sally, I thought she ruined the sale and almost gave her a spanking for it. Looking back on it now, Sally probably saved the ranch for us!" Bud was laughing when he finished the story.

"You see, Honey," said Sally, "I was a model child!"

"Not exactly, Daughter," said Bud. "What about the time we were invaded by skunks and you decided to catch one and make a house pet of him?"

"I remember that," said the cook. "She smelled up the house for days. We had to keep the windows open all the time. Pat was the only one that escaped, he was staying in the bunkhouse."

"That's right," said Pat. "The house smelled so bad, I only came in to eat to avert starvation."

"We finally called my brother Fred in and he trapped them and got rid of them somehow or other," said Bud. "We put poison out to keep them away and we haven't had a problem since. But the house smelled for weeks. I'd heard that tomato juice eliminated the skunk odor, and every night for a while I gave you a bath in tomato juice. I guess it worked, you don't smell now!" Everyone laughed.

"And," said Missus Abercrombie, "there was the time when you were at boarding school and almost caused a riot."

"I remember that," said Sally. "It was fun!"

"Fun!" thundered Bud. "I almost had to go back there and bring you home!"

"I wish you would have," said Sally.

"But you got a good education at a very prestigious, private girls' school. Very expensive also, I might add," said Bud.

"And they almost made a lady out of you," added Missus Abercrombie. "I had to complete the job!"

I asked, "Just what did she do? What happened?"

"She took a horny toad back to school one fall. I didn't know she'd caught one," said Bud. "I got a call late one night from the school administrator. She told me that my 'daughter had been misbehaving very badly, and I should seriously consider coming back there and removing her from the school.'

"I asked the administrator, 'What did she do?' The administrator told me Sally had brought a vicious, wild animal to school and turned it loose in the girls' dormitory. I asked her what kind of animal it was and the administrator told me that Sally said it was a harmless horny toad."

Bud was laughing now, almost to the point of tears.

"I didn't turn the horny toad loose," said Sally. "He got away on his own! It wasn't my fault! The administrator didn't know what a horny toad was."

"Well," continued Bud, "I called Missus Abercrombie, she spent the winters about thirty miles away, and asked her to go to the school and smooth things over, which she did, and Sally remained in school with a promise she would not bring any more wild and vicious animals back to school. I still have to laugh at a horny toad being called wild and vicious! What ever happened to that wild and vicious animal, Sally?"

"I don't know," said Sally. "I never saw him again."

"The fact that the toad got away at suppertime didn't help," said Missus Abercrombie. "It must have scared those girls almost to death!"

"I still think it was funny," said Sally.

"So," I said, "you weren't really a model child, after all, huh?"

"I was as close to being one as anyone can be," replied Sally.

Bud offered his opinion. "If the truth were known, there is no such thing as a model child. Children grow up to be adults and along the way they learn valuable lessons through their experiences, lessons that generally stay with them the rest of their lives. Some of the lessons they learn are quite humorous, some even tragic. But it's all part of growing up. You'll see as Ginny grows up. Nope, there are no model children, except my granddaughter, of course!"

Everyone laughed as Bud contradicted himself.

Bud looked around in mock astonishment. "As far as I can see, Ginny has done nothing wrong in her short life so far!"

Everyone continued to laugh as Sally said, "Daddy, it's plain to see that you're very prejudiced in favor of your granddaughter!"

"Why shouldn't I be," replied Bud. "She's my granddaughter and she really takes after me!"

"I suspect you're tryin' to tell us you were a model child," I said.

"To use Sally's words, 'I was as close to being one as anyone can be!'"

Everyone continued to laugh and Pat laughed the hardest. I had the idea that there was a lot in their childhood that hadn't been told. I decided I'd have to look into it further at a later date.

Jimmy asked, almost bashfully, but jokingly, "You mean my earlier experiences made a juvenile delinquent out of me?"

All of us knew that Jimmy had had some problems in the past and had come to the ranch at Bud's request because Bud knew his parents. When the dudes weren't around, he talked about his past freely. He was almost sent to reform school until Bud intervened.

"Jimmy," said Bud, "you had made some poor choices early which led you into making poorer and poorer choices. Now I feel like you've turned things around and you're on the right track."

"Well, then," said Jimmy, "I'm glad that I stole that kid's bike! If I hadn't, I wouldn't be here!"

Again, we all laughed. We knew how much Jimmy appreciated being on the Wilson Ranch and we knew how hard he'd worked for us and himself to turn his life around.

"Daddy," said Sally, "Ginny has fallen asleep and I think it's time we all went to bed. But I would appreciate it greatly if you would stop spoiling your granddaughter."

"I don't think that's in keeping with my duties as a grandpa," said Bud.

"Oh really?" stated Sally.

"That's right, Daughter," replied Bud. "The only thing a grandpa can do to his grandkids is spoil them! He can't spank them or punish them! He can't send them to their room for disciplinary measures! That's the parent's job! So all he can do is spoil them! And I hope I've been doing a good job!"

"You've been doing a better job than you think," retorted Sally.

"And I've succeeded! Rest assured that I'll keep trying. I'll do my best in the future! Actually, Ginny and I have become the best of friends, not to mention our grandpa and granddaughter relationship. So, I'll keep trying as hard as I can!"

Sally shrugged her shoulders in an admission of defeat and turned to go to the bedroom.

"Don't be discouraged, Daughter. Just remember your old man loves you, Ginny, and Honey very much. That's something that hasn't been said much around here, but I've tried to show it every day!"

"I know, Daddy. Goodnight," said Sally. She gave her dad a goodnight kiss and said, "Come on, Honey, it's bedtime."

Getting Ready for Fall

The next morning after breakfast we saddled our horses to take the broodmare bunch back to their range. Ginny came down and started to saddle her pony, Pumpkin. Pat and Jimmy had already gathered the mares into the big corral before breakfast.

"Just what do you think you're doing, young lady?" asked Sally.

"I'm going to help you," answered the little girl.

"Do you think you can help?" asked her mother.

"Sure," replied Ginny.

"What can you do?"

"I can help lead the horses. Pumpkin's a natural leader!"

I intervened in the question and answer session, "Can you ride at a trot for a couple of miles?"

"Sure," said Ginny.

"How do you know?"

"Grandpa's told me lots of times that I must have chased him and Dragon Slayer for ten miles around the corral!"

I turned to Sally. "Well, Darlin', I think it's time we let our little cowgirl help us!"

Ginny got excited and asked, "Does that mean I can go, Daddy?"

"That depends on what your mother says," I answered.

Sally had a look of disapproval on her face. Seeing it, I said, "I think it'll be all right. Pat an' Jimmy can follow an' you an' me can lead with Ginny. We can both keep an eye on her. I expect to go kinda slow anyway."

Still looking apprehensive, Sally said, "I guess so, if you're sure she'll be all right."

Bud said, "It'll be all right. I was taking you out when you were younger than Ginny."

I could understand Sally's reluctance to take Ginny along, Ginny was her only child.

"She'll be as safe as anybody," I said.

"I guess it's okay then," said Sally.

Ginny was elated. She gave Sally a big hug and thanked her profusely.

Before we started to take the mares back, I went to Pat and Jimmy and said, "We want to take it easy. We're takin' Ginny an' this is her first ride takin' the horses. If it takes us all day, that's okay."

"Understood," said Jimmy. Pat just nodded his head.

Bud came to the corral in the golf cart.

Ginny said, "I get to go Grandpa, just like you said!"

Sally gave her dad a look of disapproval and asked, "Did you put her up to this?"

Bud looked at Sally a little sheepishly. "I told her to go to the barn and get ready. Maybe her parents would let her go."

I laughed and checked the cinch on Pumpkin. I tightened it.

"We're ready! Get on your horse, Sis," I ordered. At my command to Ginny, everyone mounted their horses. I smiled to myself, *What a development! Everybody's answerin' to Sis now!*

"Go with your mom, Sis," I said, as I opened the gate. "An' you stay between us! Don't let any of the horses get ahead of you."

As I swung the gate open, Sally and Ginny headed out at a brisk trot. The mares followed them, a little faster than I liked. I hurried to get in front of them and slow them down, but Sally had them under control. Ginny stayed right with her, even though she had to run Pumpkin.

By the time I got around the horses and got in front of them with Sally and Ginny, they had the horses in a smooth, mile-eating trot.

As we lined out, Ginny said, "I thought we were going to leave you behind, Daddy!"

"Never, Sis, never," I said.

"That was fun," said Ginny. "I got to run Pumpkin and he stayed ahead of all the horses! I told you he was the fastest horse on the ranch."

"You've told me that more than once," I said.

We kept the trotting pace up for a few hundred yards, then slowed the pace down to a walk. The mares slowed down behind us, content to walk and graze a little along the way.

"What do you think of this job?" I asked Ginny.

"This is fun. I'm really helping, ain't I?"

"Aren't I," corrected Sally.

Ginny corrected herself. "Aren't I?" she said.

"Yep," I answered.

"That's good," said Ginny. "Grandpa said when I got big enough to help out, he'd put me on the payroll and pay me!"

"Oh really?" questioned Sally.

"Yep," replied Ginny. "He'll owe me a lot of money when we get done today!"

Sally smiled. She remembered that when she was little, Bud used to give her a dime every day she went with them on the job. She wondered, what with inflation these days, how much money her dad would give his granddaughter. She knew the dime wasn't payment for her help, she wasn't much help at the time, and it was more of a bribe to keep her out of trouble and under control. It worked, most of the time.

While keeping an eye on Ginny, Sally and I were both watching the horse herd behind us, just to make sure Pat and Jimmy weren't having any trouble. The horses were lined out pretty well, following single file or in twos and threes. Each colt followed his mom or trotted alongside her. The day was going well and I was contented to ride beside my wife and daughter.

I rode along, watching my daughter ride. She was holding up well and I was quite proud of her. I started daydreaming about how much help Ginny would be when she got bigger, and how much fun she would be. At her age now, she was still very gullible and I had a lot of fun teasing her.

100

I was jolted back to reality when I heard Pat yell in back. I turned to see a bunch of the horses in the middle of the herd running off to the west.

"Keep an eye on Ginny," I ordered Sally, as I ran my horse to head off the runaways. It was a hard job running at full speed dodging tree limbs and rocks trying to get ahead of the horses. I had no doubt Salty, the horse I was riding, could head them, it was just difficult because we had to go so much farther to get around them.

We were running at full speed when Salty stepped in a badger hole and went down. I went flying ahead of the horse and hit a large rock with my shoulder. I immediately felt a sharp pain shooting across my shoulder and down my ribs. I knew I'd busted something. I tried to get up, but only made it about halfway and fell to my knees.

Sally and Ginny had seen the whole thing and came on the run to see if they could help. I watched them and thought, *Mom, you watch your daughter!* but couldn't say anything because I had the wind knocked out of me.

Sally asked, "What happened?"

I answered, gasping for air, "I guess Salty stepped in a badger hole an' fell. Where is he?"

Ginny started to laugh. "Daddy fell off his horse!"

Sally reprimanded Ginny sharply. "Don't laugh! Can't you see Daddy's hurt?"

Ginny immediately stopped laughing as Sally started to get off her horse to see if she could help me.

"Stay on your horse," I said. "You and Ginny go back an' lead the horses to their pasture. I'll be all right. Did Pat get around them horses? Where's my horse?"

"I don't know," said Sally. "I can't see him. But Jimmy's keeping the rest of them in line."

"Good," I said. "You go lead the horses to the gate, it's only a mile, a mile an' a half farther. Pat'll just have to handle the runaways on his own. I'll wait here for you."

Reluctantly, Sally left, taking Ginny with her. I watched as they left and got ahead of the remaining horses. They continued on toward the broodmare's range.

As they passed, Jimmy started toward me to see what had happened. I tried to wave him back with my left arm, but couldn't do it. I waved him back with my right arm. He obediently returned to his position behind the horses.

I was still on my knees and took stock of my predicament. I concluded I'd broken my left shoulder, I didn't have complete mastery of my left arm, and I'd either busted some ribs or they were badly bruised. I didn't know where my horse was. I had a hard time turning around trying to look for him. I finally spotted him, about twenty yards away, grazing peacefully. I looked him over as best I could from my position and couldn't see anything wrong. He was just grazing, not favoring any leg. It appeared he had come through the wreck okay.

Presently, I heard a horse approaching. Pat came riding up.

"How bad you hurt?" he asked.

"Shoulder, arm, maybe some ribs," I answered. "Did you turn them horses back?"

"Yep, Jimmy's got them with the others."

I asked, "What spooked the horses?"

"I dunno," answered Pat. "There might have been a bear or a mountain lion in the trees. I didn't see. It could have been some elk suddenly moving, I just don't know."

"Well," I said, "get my horse. I'll have to find a rock or something to use to get on. You might have to help me."

Pat laughed. "I can do that! You know I've been helping dudes get on for years!"

Even though it hurt, I couldn't help but laugh.

Pat brought my horse over. I watched him walk. There was no sign of a limp or any other injury.

"I'll have to get on from the off side," I said. "My left arm is plumb useless."

"Get on that big rock. You should be able to get on without much trouble from there."

I made it to the rock Pat pointed out and stopped to catch my breath. The pain was almost unbearable. Pat helped me up on the rock and positioned Salty to where I could just swing over into the saddle.

Seated in the saddle, I said, "Well, I'm ready. Let's go find our riders."

"No," said Pat, we need to start toward the ranch. Our riders can catch up to us."

Meekly I agreed and we started toward the ranch. I couldn't look back over my left shoulder to see where our riders were, and it was very painful to look over my right shoulder. Pat noticed this and said, "I'll keep an eye out for 'em and let you know when they catch up."

Pat and I had made it about halfway back to the ranch when Sally, Ginny, and Jimmy caught up to us.

"How bad are you hurt?" asked Sally when they arrived.

"My shoulder, arm, and ribs seem to be affected," I said, trying to downplay how painful it really was.

"I'm sorry I laughed," said Ginny.

"That's okay, Sis. All cowboys laugh when they see someone fall off. They laugh until they find out he's okay, then they keep laughing. When they find out he's hurt, they stop laughing. Of course, in the dude business, we're not supposed to laugh when someone falls off, especially a dude."

"I'm sorry anyway," said Ginny

"That just proves you're a real cowboy," I said.

"Cowgirl!" corrected Ginny. Everyone laughed.

"I stand corrected," I said.

The ride back to the ranch was slow due to my condition and Ginny was getting tired.

"You'll have to come to town with me tonight," said Sally. "We'll bring Missus Abercrombie. I'll take you to the hospital first, then take Missus Abercrombie and Ginny home so Ginny can go to bed—she has school in the morning—then come back and check on you."

I didn't argue. I knew my situation was serious enough that it required a doctor's attention.

When we reached the ranch, I rode to the mounting block to get off. Bud noticed this and came to the corrals.

"What happened?" Sally told the story.

When I'd gotten off, Jimmy came and got my horse. "I'll take care of him," he said.

Through the pain, I managed to utter, "Thanks."

Ginny said, "I'll take care of Pumpkin."

"I'll take care of your horse, Sally," said Pat. "You all go get something to eat so you can get to town."

Sally said, "Thanks Pat, I really appreciate it!" It is the custom on most all ranches that a hand takes care of his own horse. Of course, the dudes weren't expected to take care of their own horses. Our help was treating my wife and me as dudes or wealthy owners. However, I had to remember that it was due to my condition that we were receiving such preferential treatment.

Bud, Sally, Ginny, Missus Abercrombie, and I were eating when Pat and Jimmy came in to eat. I was having a difficult time and Sally had to cut the meat for me. I tried to object, but Sally said, "That's all right, I'm used to doing it for Ginny!"

Everyone laughed and I felt a little embarrassed.

"The evening chores are done," Pat reported.

When we finished, Sally went to get me an extra set of clothes and we made ready to go to town.

Before we got to the door, Ginny cried, "We can't leave yet. I haven't taken care of Pumpernickel!"

"Pumpernickel! Who's that? We don't have a horse named Pumpernickel," said Bud.

"Pumpernickel is my new horse. That's what I've named him," said Ginny.

"Don't worry about Pumpernickel," said Jimmy, listening from the dinner table. "I've already fed him and I gave him some extra feed."

The trip to town was slow. Sally was concerned about my comfort. Her concern was justified, as I couldn't get comfortable.

By the time we reached the hospital, both Ginny and Missus

Abercrombie were asleep in the backseat. When we stopped the car, Missus Abercrombie woke up, but Ginny continued to sleep.

As I slowly made my way into the hospital, Sally joined me. "I asked Missus Abercrombie to watch Ginny while I checked you in," she said. "We'll get you checked in, I'll take them home and put Ginny in bed, then come back to see how you're doing."

"You don't have to come back," I said. "You belong with Ginny. There's nothing you can do here anyway."

"But I belong with you. Ginny will be all right."

The nurse on duty saw the way I was holding my shoulder and said, "Broken shoulder. Sit in this wheelchair, we'll go for some X-rays."

"I'd rather walk." I said.

"Sit!" ordered the nurse. "Our liability."

Gingerly, I sat down. I didn't see Sally leave, but heard her say, "I'll be back."

The doctor showed up while the X-rays were being taken. When they were developed, the doctor said, "We should probably operate and remove these bone splinters. They'll cause you some problems in the future if we don't. We can put a screw in there to help hold it in place while it's healing. Do you consent to that?"

"Whatever you say, you're the doc."

"Then sign these release forms and we'll prepare you for surgery."

I signed the papers and the nurse helped me take off my shirt. It was really painful, even though the nurse tried to be gentle. We finally got the shirt off.

"Now your pants," said the nurse.

"My pants! Why!"

"You're going into a sterile room. We can't have it contaminated with all that, ah … ah …" The nurse was searching for the right words to describe the horse manure that had been splattered on my britches.

"Ah, shall we say, corral dust? We don't want to risk infection."

"That'll work," I said. "You'll have to help me unbuckle my belt. I can't hardly use my left arm."

The nurse obliged and I was embarrassed that I couldn't take off my own pants. After she unbuckled my belt, she gave me one of those hospital gowns that only covers up part of a person.

I looked at it and said, "That ain't goin' to keep me very warm," I said.

"It's not supposed to," said the nurse. "Get on that gurney and we'll go to surgery."

I had trouble getting on the gurney. When I finally did, the nurse didn't waste any time wheeling me into the operating room.

"We'll put you to sleep and pretty soon you won't feel anything," said the doctor. "Give him the IV, Raymond."

I remember asking, "Whose Raymond?" but fell asleep and didn't hear the answer.

I woke up sometime later. I don't know how long I was out. Sally was asleep in a chair next to my bed. The sun was starting to come up. My shoulder still hurt and I tried to roll over, but couldn't. Sally heard me stirring and woke up.

"How are you feeling?"

"Miserable," I answered. "What time is it?"

"It's early morning," replied Sally.

"You need to get Ginny to school." My mind was starting to clear.

"Missus Abercrombie will take Ginny to school."

"Good. Then you can take me back to the ranch an' I'll get back to work."

"Very funny," said Sally. "The doctor said you'd need to stay here a day or two. He wants to monitor how your shoulder is healing. He says he dug quite a few bone fragments out of your shoulder."

"I can't just stay here," I protested. "There's things that need to be done at the ranch!"

"Nothing that Jimmy and Pat can't handle. We do have a few guests coming, just for weekend stays, but they'll be taken care of when we get back next Friday night."

"How do you know?"

"Because I'll be there," replied Sally. "And you'll be there also. By the way, I called your folks and let them know you'd had an accident, but were expected to be all right. Your mother said she'd try to get out here to see you, but didn't make any promises."

"She don't have to come," I said.

"She did say she'd like to see Ginny and me," said Sally.

"That's it!" I said. "Other motives!" I was trying to have some fun with Sally because she seemed to be taking this situation too seriously.

"The doctor said that with proper exercise and physical therapy you should regain the full use of your left arm in time. He said there was some nerve damage. And he said it looked like there had been some previous damage. Have you hurt it before?"

I immediately thought of the bareback bronc that had bucked me off at the rodeo I was entered in when my horse, Roman, and my donkey were stolen. I'd hurt my shoulder, but couldn't remember which one. I remembered now.

Answering her question, I simply said, "Yes." Then I responded to her previous statement about regaining full use of my arm. "Hah! I'll use it before you know it!" I tried to move my left arm, but couldn't—it was bandaged to my left side.

The doctor came in. "How are you feeling?"

"Oh, just fine," I said sarcastically. Actually I was still a little lightheaded from the anesthetic. "What's this about regaining full use of my arm in time?"

The doctor said, "In addition to knocking the ball out of the socket in your shoulder, you splintered your shoulder blade. We had quite a time getting all the bone fragments out of your shoulder. There may have been some nerve damage. We'll need to keep you here for observation for a few days."

"But I need to get back to the ranch. We're makin' plans for the fall, an' ..."

The doctor interrupted. "Did you plan that fall?"

"Certainly not!" I said.

Sensing that he might have a somewhat cantankerous patient on his hands, the doctor said, "You just need to rest here and do what you're told and you'll be okay. Besides that, you can't leave until I release you and if you give me a problem I'll demand full payment before you leave!" He thought a second, then added, "IN CASH!"

Sally was quietly enjoying this talking to that the doctor was giving me and I could see her trying to stifle her laugh.

"Okay, Doc," I said. "I'll be the best ..." I paused a moment remembering Sally's statement that she was a "model child," and added, "model prisoner ... ah, that is model patient you ever had."

The doctor smiled and turned to leave. "I'll hold you to that," he said, and left.

After the doctor was gone, Sally started to laugh. "I guess he told you!"

I didn't have anything to say, other than, "Everyone's takin' advantage of an invalid!"

The nurse came in and said, "The doctor ordered that I give you a shot to help with the pain and ..."

"Help with the pain!" I hollered. "The pain don't need no help!"

The nurse smiled. "This shot will kill the pain."

"I don't need it," I said. "I'm half afraid the shot will kill me!"

"It won't kill you," said the nurse, "but it might make you a little drowsy."

"You'll put me to sleep," I said, "then forget to come in here an' wake me up!" I was trying to have a little fun with the nurse, but not succeeding. At least Sally was amused at my antics.

The nurse turned toward her and asked, "Is he always like this?"

Sally, smiling, replied, "Not always. Sometimes he's worse! I think the drugs you have him on are having a positive effect."

The nurse gave Sally a funny look, gave me the shot and left.

Sally asked, "Is there anything I can get for you? I need to be going to make sure Ginny got to school all right and start work on our sale catalog."

"Maybe something to read and a reprieve," I answered.

Sally smiled, gave me a kiss and left. I promptly fell asleep again.

During the next few days, I became very irritable and discontented. I really didn't have anything to do. I slept a lot. I read a lot, but soon tired of it. And I was very restless, but couldn't move around very much, being bandaged as I was. I couldn't see that the doctors were doing anything and I couldn't see how I was improving. The bandages were changed every day, and that was a relief, but I still couldn't move my arm without a great deal of pain. I thought the bandaging was worse than the injury, but the doctor and nurses had stressed, "Keep still or it won't heal properly!" Every other day or so, they took X-rays.

My mother didn't show up. She called and said there was too much going on at our ranch and they couldn't get away. She said maybe they could make it over the holidays. It was just as well, as irritable as I was, I wouldn't be very good company.

Finally, the doctor came in with Sally. "I think we can let you go now. There's not much more we can do for you."

When he said that, I thought to myself, *There's not much you have done for me!*

The doctor continued, "That shoulder seems to be healing properly, but it's absolutely essential you keep it still. The nurse will show your wife how to bandage it when she changes the bandage. Keep it on twenty-four hours a day, and come back in a week."

The doctor left and the nurse and Sally changed the bandage. Then the nurse took off the bandage and had Sally bandage it again, just to make sure she knew how to do it. The nurse said, "There's not really a good way to immobilize a shoulder. This is the best we can do."

I felt like a guinea pig.

Sally and I left to pick up Ginny from school so we could get back to the ranch. Ginny had been to visit me in the hospital after school when Sally came. It had been nice to see her, but I was disappointed I couldn't set her on my knee. On the way to the ranch, I sat in the backseat and Ginny rode in the front. I think she felt really grown up riding in the front.

Missus Abercrombie stayed at the house in town, saying she had some things to do.

As we drove, Sally said, "I'll have to bring Ginny back to school, but I'll show Rachel how to change the bandage and she can handle it. Ginny and I will be back Friday night and check on you."

"I'll have to check on Pumpernickel," said Ginny.

I laughed. It was the first time I'd laughed in a week. I was starting to feel better.

We arrived at the ranch just as everyone was finishing eating. The cook had saved us something to eat, as Sally had called and informed him we were coming but that we'd be late.

Ginny couldn't wait to ask Jimmy, "How's Pumpernickel?"

"Pumpernickel is doing just fine," said Jimmy. "I've been taking extra special good care of him, just for you!"

After the initial "Hello's" and "How you doing?" we sat down to eat. Sally cut my steak into bite-sized portions so I could eat. I really felt kinda childish, having this done for me, but I couldn't use my left arm. I'd done it for Ginny plenty of times.

While we were eating, the talk turned to the upcoming fall gather of the cows.

"Looks like it'll just be Jimmy and me," said Pat. "It shouldn't be too rough, the cold weather will bring a lot of the cattle down."

"I can leave Ginny in town with Missus Abercrombie," said Sally. "I'll be able to help out for a week."

"That'll help," said Pat, knowing how good a hand Sally is. "But it will still be a lot of riding. We'll manage, one way or another."

I felt uncomfortable. I wouldn't be able to help with the gather and that meant extra work for everyone else.

Bud asked, "What do you expect to do out here, Honey?"

"I don't think there's much I can do, other than get in everybody's way," I said. Everyone laughed.

"Well," said Bud, "seeing as you can't do much, you can ride around with me in the golf cart or four-wheeler and supervise. You're still the boss here, and maybe you can improve your supervising skills!" Again, everyone laughed.

"That may not work," I said.

Jimmy asked, "How come?"

"I've never asked or told anyone to do somethin' I wouldn't or couldn't do myself," I said. "Right now, I can't do anythin', so it wouldn't be right to tell anyone to do somethin'."

"That's great! We won't have to do anything at all," said Jimmy.

Again, everyone laughed, knowing Jimmy was only kidding. But Jimmy was on a roll and he continued, "That's what I've always wanted, an all-expense paid vacation on a dude ranch! And for an unlimited time!"

Laughing, Bud said, "We may have to analyze your thinking, Jimmy."

Pat and Jimmy went to the bunkhouse and everyone else made ready to go to bed.

Before Bud went to his room, he told Sally, "We have a family coming out for the weekend. They'll only be here tomorrow night and leave Sunday afternoon."

"I'm glad to see that you're making some money while I'm gone," said Sally.

"Pat knows what to do," I said. "This crew doesn't need much supervisin'," I said, referring to Bud's earlier comments.

"True," said Bud, "but every now and then, you can see something that could use a little adjustment to make things run a little better."

Ginny had to be assured that Pumpernickel would be all right until she could see him in the morning before she went to bed.

Unexpected Help

The next day, Sally, Pat, and Jimmy ran the saddle horses in. As usual, they came in at a full gallop, and I was missing out on the action. I sat on the front porch of the lodge, drinking my coffee with a warm coat on. Bud was with me.

"I miss that," said Bud.

"Me too," I stated.

"Well," said Bud, "now you'll have a chance to see what I've been going through the last few years."

"You know," I said, "I don't really envy you an' your situation. But I do admire the way you've adjusted to it an' the way you cope with it. I'm not so sure I could live with it."

"You're getting a chance to find out now," said Bud, laughing a little.

"I guess you're right," I said, laughing a little myself. "How do you do it?"

"Well," answered Bud, turning a little serious, "I had to learn to accept my situation for just what it was. There sure wasn't anything I could do to change it. Then, I had to figure out how I could make the most of what had happened. I didn't really learn how to do that, I'm still learning. But life is certainly worthwhile now!"

At the risk of being cynical, I asked, "How do you figure?"

"First off," replied Bud, "look at the beautiful granddaughter you and Sally have given me! I've had a lot of fun with that youngster and we've …"

"Chasin' Pumpkin around the corral with Dragon Killer?" I interrupted. I remembered Ginny's story. "An' killin' fire-breathin' dragons?"

Bud laughed. "Dragon Slayer," he corrected. "Yes, and we've become the best of buddies. If I hadn't been in this wheelchair, I might not have devised those games with Ginny. I probably would have been out with the dudes and horses and wouldn't have had the time to spend with her. She's a pretty smart little gal and she reminds me a lot of Sally when she was younger. Even though I've been in this chair, Ginny has made it more than bearable. And now you're going to have another one! I sure am excited and hope it's a boy!"

"A boy would be nice, but a little sister for Ginny would be nice, too," I said.

Our conversation was interrupted as Sally, Pat, and Jimmy arrived at the lodge. The "good morning" greetings went around.

Sally asked, "Is Ginny up yet?"

"Yes," answered Bud. "She was all ready to go down and check Pumpernickel, but I made her eat her breakfast."

"Thank you," said Sally. "Sometimes I think she minds you better than me."

Everyone went in to eat breakfast. I hobbled in behind them. Breakfast wasn't difficult, I could cut everything with my fork. At supper, Sally had to cut the meat into bite-sized portions for me, and I felt very helpless.

As soon as Jimmy finished eating, he volunteered to take Ginny down to the barn to check on Pumpernickel. She was ready and they stayed down at the barn until the weekenders, as we called short-term guests, arrived.

Our weekenders were a middle-aged couple taking a weekend vacation to celebrate their tenth wedding anniversary. They didn't have any children and took to Ginny immediately. Bud and Sally greeted them, but I felt uncomfortable in my condition meeting strangers.

There wasn't much I could do, other than offer a feeble, "Welcome, we're glad you're here."

They noticed my condition and Ginny volunteered, "Daddy

fell off his horse!" The ranch crew laughed. The guests expressed concern, but didn't say a lot.

The guests were shown to their cabin and Sally made arrangements for them to go on an afternoon ride.

"Ginny," said Sally, "do you want to guide the ride after dinner? It will be your first guided ride."

"Sure, Mommy," replied Ginny. "Can we go to my favorite spot?"

"Where's that?" asked Sally.

"Up where all the family is buried."

"No," said Sally, "that's a private spot and we don't take our guests up there. Let's go up on the ridge where we can get a pretty view of the whole country."

"But it's pretty at my favorite spot," argued Ginny.

"No," said Sally adamantly. "If you head up there, I'll take the lead."

Ginny consented, reluctantly.

After the noon meal, Pat and Jimmy got horses for the guests and got them mounted. Sally gave some instructions on how to handle their horses and ended up by saying, "Ginny is going to lead this ride. It will be her first time guiding and I hope she doesn't get us lost!"

The guests laughed and Ginny retorted, "I won't get us lost, Mommy!"

The riders left. They were expected to be gone for an hour and a half or so. Pat and Jimmy were busy repairing tack. The cook was busy baking a cake for the guest's anniversary celebration. It would be a little surprise for them. Bud was busy looking over the rough draft of the sale catalog Sally had prepared while she was in town. I didn't have anything to do.

Bud noticed that I was bored and said, "Do you want to look over this sale catalog? I really don't need to approve anything Sally does, I think she seeks my approval just to kinda keep me involved."

I agreed. Only half interested, I looked the catalog over. It appeared to be fine.

"I think Sally can get it printed just the way it is," said Bud.

"She can get them mailed out next week. I hope we have a good turnout for our sale."

After about two hours, I became concerned. The riders hadn't returned yet. The memory of my accident was still fresh in my mind and I hoped nothing had happened.

Presently, I saw them coming through the trees about half a mile away. They were all horseback and none of the horses seemed to be favoring a leg as they walked. Satisfied that everything appeared to be all right, I walked down to the corrals to wait for them.

Pat and Jimmy saw me walking slowly to the corrals and Jimmy asked, "Coming down to check up on us?"

His comment was made good-naturedly and I didn't take offense, although I was acutely aware of my supervisory position and aware that supervising was all I could do.

"Yes," I said. "I thought you guys might be working too hard down here an' I came down to make you take a break!"

Pat laughed. "Your concern for our welfare is impressive," he said.

"You don't have to make me take a break," said Jimmy. "I've been working real slow on this so I'll have something to do tomorrow!" We all laughed.

Soon the riders arrived, with Ginny still in the lead.

"Did you get lost, Ginny?" I asked. "You're late gettin' back."

"No, I didn't get lost," said Ginny. She said it in a manner that implied she was insulted. "Mister and Missus Garrett were enjoying the ride and they wanted to stay out longer, so we stayed out longer."

Sally was listening and I saw her nodding her head in approval.

Ginny got off her horse and tied him up. Pat and Jimmy helped the Garrett's off their horses and Sally took care of her horse.

"Do you want to see Pumpernickel?" Ginny asked the Garrett's.

"Why yes," answered Mister Garrett.

"Follow me," said Ginny, as she walked toward the corral where her colt was. "You can't go in the corral, but I'll catch him and bring him over to you. He's still just a baby and might not be used to strangers yet."

"Your daughter certainly has a gift of gab," said Sally. "She talked all the time, mostly about her horse, Pumpernickel, and how she was going to break him and how good a horse he was going to be. I asked the Garrett's if they were getting tired of the ride and Ginny's talk, but they said they weren't. They said they were actually enjoying it."

"That's good," I said.

"I need to tell Ginny that she should ask a few questions of the guests and listen to their answers. I'm sure they don't want to listen to her talk about herself all the time. The Garrett's will go for a ride tomorrow morning, then leave in the afternoon," said Sally. "Ginny and I will also leave tomorrow afternoon. I've been thinking. You have a doctor's appointment Friday. I'll come out Thursday and take you to town in the afternoon, then bring you and Ginny back here Friday after your doctor's appointment and school." Sally said this in a matter of fact tone and I knew her mind was made up.

"If Daddy likes the sale catalog, I'll have it printed during the week and start mailing them out," she continued. "Can you think of anything else I need to do while I'm in town?"

"We do need to get 'NO HUNTING' signs," I said.

"How many?"

"Better get about fifty. We'll go all the way around the ranch."

"Anything else?"

"Not that I can think of."

Ginny led the Garrett's on another ride the next morning. Before they left, Ginny said to me, "Don't worry, Daddy. If Mister and Missus Garrett want to stay out longer, we'll stay out longer. And Mommy will be along."

"Now that you've told me," I said, "I won't worry."

I was proud of my daughter. Her comment to me about staying out longer showed me that she was becoming more responsible.

The riders left and once again, I didn't have anything to do. I went into the barn to visit with Pat and Jimmy while they repaired tack. I tried to help, but there wasn't anything I could do with my arm wrapped up like it was.

Within a couple of hours, the riders returned. They told me

that they'd had a good ride. After the noon meal, while the Garretts prepared to leave, Mister Garrett told Sally, "We'd like to come back again next year, about this same time. Would that be possible?"

They were in the office and Sally looked at the reservation board on the wall for next year. It was pretty full for the summer months, but there was a lot of room available toward the end of September. "Certainly," she said, "when would you like to come?"

Mister Garrett gave Sally the dates, then said, "We'd like to stay a few days longer. Would that be possible?"

"We could certainly arrange that," said Sally. She wrote down the dates on the board.

Then Mister Garrett asked, "What is our bill for the last two days?"

Sally said, "You've only been here one night. You've had two horseback rides and meals. Of course, it's off-season, so we won't charge you the full rate. You'll save a little money." She totaled the bill and told him the amount.

"And what about a deposit for next year?" asked Mister Garrett.

Sally told him and he made out a check. As he handed it to her, he said, "There's a little extra for Ginny. A tip. She's a sweet kid. We really enjoyed our ride with her. Will she be here next year?"

"She'll be here on the weekends," said Sally. "She has school, you know."

Sally looked at the check Mister Garrett had made out. "This is quite a big tip for Ginny. Are you sure you want to give her this much?"

Missus Garrett had finished packing and entered the room. "Yes," said Missus Garrett. "For the last two days, she has taken the place of the child we couldn't have."

"I understand," said Sally. "However, I won't tell her how much you've given her. I'll give her a dollar. She'll be pleased to get it— she'll probably spend it on candy—and I'll put the rest in a savings account for her. She can use it when she gets older."

"A mother with some sense," said Mister Garrett. "I'm sure she will put it to good use someday."

The Garretts got ready to leave. Ginny was present to say good-bye and invite them back, as Sally had instructed.

Mister Garrett said, "By the way, Ginny, we've left a little something for you with your mom."

"A surprise?" asked Ginny.

"Sort of," replied Mister Garrett.

"What is it, Mommy?"

Winking at Mister Garrett, Sally reached in her pocket and pulled out a dollar bill and gave it to Ginny. "This is all yours," she said.

"Wow!" exclaimed Ginny. "A whole dollar! Can I spend it on anything I want to?"

"Yes, when we get to town."

Ginny was pleased. "I'll buy some candy bars for me and some sugar cubes for Pumpernickel! Thank you, Mister Garrett!" She gave the Garrett's both a big hug and they smiled broadly as they left.

Later that afternoon, Sally and Ginny left for town. Before they left, I advised Ginny that it would be better to get Pumpernickel some horse treats rather than sugar cubes.

"You might find Pumpernickel biting your shirt lookin' for sugar," I said.

"But a dollar isn't enough to buy horse treats," said Ginny.

"Then save your money until you have enough for horse treats."

"Can I still buy a candy bar?" asked Ginny.

"That's up to you," I answered.

I resigned myself to staying around the lodge and answering the phone. I drank more coffee in the morning than what I needed, but there wasn't much I could do. I was relieved when Thursday came and Sally took me to town.

Before we left for town, she gave Bud a copy of the sale catalog and left a box of them at the ranch. I grabbed a catalog to look through on our ride to town. She'd also had some single sheet flyers printed up announcing our sale.

On Friday, we went to the doctor's. X-rays were taken of my shoulder and the doctor said, "Your shoulder and arm seem to be healing normally. I think we can leave the bandage off. You'll need to exercise that arm and shoulder for a while."

The doctor took me down to the physical therapy room and introduced me to the therapist. "You do what he tells you and you'll have full use of that arm and shoulder before long."

"How long?" I asked.

"That depends on how well you do the exercises," replied the doctor. "This is John, our physical therapist. You'll need to come back in about two weeks for a checkup and you can also check in with John while you're here."

We shook hands and John looked over my shoulder. "The doc informed me of your situation. The bones seem to be healing normally, so we need to concentrate on building back the muscle. You can start by squeezing a rubber ball on a regular basis." He gave me a rubber ball then he showed me some exercises to do with my arm that would strengthen my shoulder and arm. When I did them, it hurt like the dickens.

John saw the pain on my face, smiled and said, "It will hurt for a while. Those muscles have been injured and, not being used for a while, they're reluctant to work. You do each one of these exercises for at least fifteen minutes each morning and each evening. You can do them periodically during the day. It will hurt for a while, but you should notice the pain becoming less each day. The more you do them, the less it will hurt and that will show that the muscles are regaining their strength."

The exercises were simple. In addition to squeezing the ball, they consisted of moving my arm in a circular manner around vertically and horizontally. I was to reach down with my left arm and touch my right toes. At John's order, I did each exercise for fifteen minutes before he would let me go.

Before I left, John said, "Remember, you're supposed to do each exercise at least fifteen minutes in the morning and evening. When you come back in two weeks, we'll see how much your range of motion has improved. Don't lift anything heavy with that arm for a while."

119

Sally had been waiting for me after she'd filled out the release forms and we left the hospital.

"What do we do now?" I asked.

"I've got the 'NO HUNTING' signs picked up. We could drive around town and post these sale flyers at the feed stores and wherever. That would keep us busy until school's out."

"Let's do it," I said. "I've been idle too long an' although it's next to doin' nothin', it's still somethin' to do. It beats squeezin' this ball all day!"

Sally drove to the feed stores and we posted the flyers. At each stop, I was greeted by the owners or managers and asked, "We heard you had a wreck, what happened?"

A simple reply, "My horse fell with me," seemed to satisfy everyone. A few folks asked, "Are you all right?"

"Will be," was my short reply. I wasn't used to being the center of attention and news travels fast in a small town.

We posted a few at the saddle shop and I spent some time visiting with the owner. At his insistence, I had to give a more detailed description of what happened and what I was going through. When I got done, he said, "I had about the same thing happen to me. It about put me out of commission. I never did regain the full use of my arm. You do them exercises regularly and you'll be okay."

The saddle shop owner was an old cowboy. I'd noticed he seemed to favor his right arm, but had never asked him about it.

When school was out, we picked up Ginny and drove to the ranch. I started feeling better when we left town, even though I knew I couldn't do much at the ranch.

The weekend went well. We had a few overnighters and Ginny and Sally took those people that wanted to for a ride. I wasn't much help, but I could move around a little easier without the bandages. Sunday night, Sally and Ginny returned to town.

I spent a lot of time doing my exercises. It was still painful, but the pain was becoming less each day. At least it gave me something to do.

Thursday, I was sitting on the porch in the afternoon, halfheartedly doing my exercises, soaking up the sun, when I noticed a rider leading a packhorse approaching the ranch. The horse he was riding looked familiar, but I couldn't place the rider. Bud noticed the rider from inside the lodge and joined me on the porch.

"Do you recognize him?" asked Bud.

"No," I said. "But the horse looks strangely familiar. Kinda resembles Pat's ol' horse, the one he gave to Mud."

"That's him!" exclaimed Bud. "Dusty Waters! Mud! The old codger has finally showed up. Honey, go down to the barn and get Pat! We've got a visitor!"

I started toward the barn, but Pat and Jimmy were already headed toward the lodge. I met them halfway.

"We've got a visitor that you know," I said.

"I know," said Pat, "I saw him from the barn."

We went back to the lodge and waited for Mud to show up. He rode up to the porch and greeted us with a simple, "Howdy."

"Howdy, Mud!" Bud seemed pleased to see him. "How come you haven't shown up earlier?"

"There wasn't no need to show up earlier," said Mud.

"Well," said Bud. "Fall off your horse and come tell us what you've been up to!"

"Don't fall!" I admonished. Pat chuckled.

Mud got off his horse, tied him at the hitch rail, and came up on the porch. After hearty handshakes and a lot of pats on the back, and an introduction of Jimmy, Bud asked, "What brings you up this way?"

"I used to know your father, Jimmy. How is he?"

"Fine," answered Jimmy, surprised that Mud was acquainted with his father.

Turning to Bud, Mud said, "Your brother, Fred, was down my way making a deer count or something and told me your top hand, Honey, had got laid up. I thought you could use some extra help gatherin' your cattle, so I rode up. Besides, I figure I owe you for helping put that renegade bull out of commission. He did a lot of damage to your truck. I brought my bedroll, I'm ready to stay for the duration."

"We can sure use the extra help," said Bud. "But Honey's a pretty good hand, I'm not sure you can replace him."

Mud smiled. "I didn't come to replace him. I just come to be of some help."

Bud and Pat smiled. Bud said, "Pat will show you where to put up your horses and where to put your bedroll. I'll tell the cook to fix some extra for supper."

Pat, Jimmy, and Mud went to the barn and Bud went to the kitchen. I was left alone on the porch and did feel some relief. Extra help meant less work for Pat, Jimmy, and Sally during the fall gather. I wouldn't be much help, but I figured on getting horseback some and doing what I could.

When Pat, Jimmy, and Mud returned to the lodge, Bud had come out on the porch and joined me. The cook also came out. There was a big reunion on that porch, as the cook had also known Mud earlier. Jimmy and I were largely ignored as the old timers rehashed the old days. I listened carefully, anxious to pick up some of the history of these old cowboys.

I heard Bud say, "I ought to call George, Jimmy's father, and invite him out here to have a proper reunion. He can bring Jimmy's mother and stay in one of the cabins."

Jimmy said, "He might even be able to help out some."

"Probably," said Pat. "He's a better cowboy than what you might suspect, Jimmy."

Jimmy looked surprised. He had very little knowledge of his father's cowboy experience.

"Yep," said Bud, directing his comments toward Jimmy. "The five of us, your dad, the cook, Mud, Pat and myself, we had some hair-raising times chasing wild horses and gathering cattle."

Pat, Mud, and the cook chuckled. Bud continued, "I heard you had your leg cut off, Mud. Can you still ride?"

"Not like I used to," said Mud. "I need a pretty gentle horse nowadays, like the one Pat gave me. It's kinda tough gettin' on and off."

"How's your horse that got gored?" asked Pat.

"He died," said Mud. "I pumped him full of antibiotics, but it didn't seem to help. I probably should have shot him right then and there, put him out of his misery, but he'd been an honest, faithful partner. I had to do what I had to do. He'd never let me down, so I had to try. Besides that, I've had to shoot too many horses lately," referring to the fact that he'd shot our stud.

Bud didn't refer to Mud's shooting our stud, but said, "That's too bad. But we've got plenty of horses here. You'll be well mounted while you're helping us."

"I figured," said Mud.

Pat asked, "How's my old saddle horse working out for you?"

"Great," said Mud. "He's as honest as the day is long."

"Remember," said Pat, "if you let him set too long, he's liable to buck after a rest. And he can do a good job of it!"

At supper that night, Bud explained to Mud our plan of action. "We have our annual horse sale coming up in a few weeks. We'll need to gather the mares we've decided to sell, along with their colts and some yearlings and get them ready to sell. It'll be pretty tough making them look good, they've already started growing their winter coats. We'll sell a few of the older dude horses, Honey still has to pick them out, and a few of the two-year-olds. Come sale day, we'll be pretty busy.

"After the sale, we'll start gathering cows. As nice as the weather's been, the cattle will be pretty well scattered. A few of the older cows will come down of their own accord, but there'll be plenty of riding to gather them all. When we've got all of them, we'll wean the calves, sort the steers from the heifers, sort the longhorns from the others, then go through the cows and do some culling. We'll need to preg check the cows and sell the open ones. When we've decided how many cows to cull, we'll sort the heifers as to what we want to keep for replacements and sell the rest. We'll also have to cull some bulls."

"Sounds like there's a lot of corral work," said Mud.

"There is, there is," said Bud, "but we should get through it pretty quick. We've got a good set of corrals to work in. We expect to hold our cattle sale along in the middle of November. If you can help out until then, I'll pay you top wages! Then …"

123

"You don't need to pay me," interrupted Mud, "I figure you got it comin'."

Bud looked at Mud in surprise. "Well," he continued, "we'll talk about that later. I was going to say that if you wanted to work through the winter, we could probably use you. I don't know how fast Honey is going to recover and we could use more help."

I wanted to say that "I'd be better before he knew it," but I kept quiet.

"Jimmy's going back to school after the first of the year," continued Bud, "and that leaves Honey, Pat, the cook, and me to take care of things during the winter. I'm useless, the cook prefers to stay in the kitchen, and he likes it warm! That just leaves Pat and Honey, with Sally on the weekends. There's a lot of feeding to do, and Honey has the replacement heifer program to deal with in the spring. What are your chores down at your place?"

"I've got plenty to do down there during the winter," said Mud. "What horses do you have for an old invalid to ride?" I could tell Mud was getting uncomfortable discussing the upcoming winter plans.

It appeared to me that Mud wasn't willing to stay during the winter. I made a mental note to have Sally, when she came out for the weekend, put an ad in the "Help Wanted" section of the paper to get another man or two to help us through the winter.

"Mud can use any of my horses," I said. "Although I'd prefer that Roman an' Drygulch not be used. They're startin' to show some age an' I'd like to take it easy on 'em. They might be good for some small circles though. That one colt, Mistake, he's liable to buck, it's been so long since he's been used."

"We've got plenty of horses, we shouldn't have to use yours, Honey," said Pat.

I figured Pat was planning on using the dude horses for Mud. He'd seen him ride when we were trying to corral that maverick bull, and I thought Pat figured he couldn't ride too good with that artificial leg. That was all right, we had a lot of good horses in the dude string.

The talk among the four old timers went well into the night.

Jimmy left early and went to bed. I stuck around a little longer, then hit the sack myself.

The following morning found everyone up at the usual time, seemingly unaffected by staying up late into the night. Pat and Jimmy ran in the saddle horses, and after breakfast Pat took Mud to the corral to pick out the horses he could use. He picked out four horses and his horse knowledge became apparent—he picked out good ones.

Pat asked, "Do you know those horses now?"

Mud replied, "I picked 'em, didn't I?"

Pat said, "We could tie a handkerchief to the mane of each horse so you won't forget them." Pat was teasing Mud.

"Ha!" replied Mud. "You've been in the dude business too long! I ain't a wet-nosed kid that don't know what he's doing!"

Pat laughed. "I forgot," he said.

The fall days dragged on slowly. Jimmy took care of Pumpernickel morning and night. The colt had gentled down considerably and I had no qualms about Ginny being around him without adult supervision. I continued doing my exercises and the pain was becoming less. I was confident I would regain full use of my arm. I could feel the strength coming back, but it wasn't coming fast enough.

Pat took Mud out for a couple of rides to acquaint him with the country around the ranch. I wanted to tell them that "we don't do any dude rides this time of year durin' the middle of the week," but didn't. I didn't want to offend Mud. I did give the NO HUNTING signs to Pat and he and Mud posted them on the boundary fences.

Friday came and late that night, Sally, Ginny, and Missus Abercrombie arrived. Missus Abercrombie hadn't been at the ranch for a couple of weeks and I was pleased to see her. Apparently, she was pleased to see Mud, although Mud seemed to be a little uncomfortable in her presence.

The following day, George McIntyre, Jimmy's father, and his mother showed up. Jimmy showed them to a cabin that Rachel had prepared for them. There was another reunion between the five old timers on the porch that day. It wasn't as involved as the previous one, as we had some weekend guests that needed attention. As usual, Missus McIntyre had brought out plenty of jams and jellies.

That afternoon it started to lightly snow. "This might help bring our cows down," I said to Sally.

"Yes," she replied, "but it will be cold."

"By the way," I said, "we need to put an ad in the paper for some extra help this winter. Bud offered Mud a job, but I don't think he'll take it."

"I've already done that," said Sally.

"When?"

"While you were in the hospital. Daddy said we ought to start looking for more help because he didn't know how long you'd be laid up. Even if you recover enough to work this winter, we still need to get some more help. We've got a lot of cows and horses to feed."

I asked, "Have you had any response to the ad?"

"Not really," said Sally, "just a couple of drifters and drunks. Nobody I thought we would want to hire. When a likely prospect shows up, I'll send him out to you for interviews. You need to come to town Thursday for your doctor's appointment on Friday. I'll come and pick you up, just like last time."

"I don't deserve a chauffeured ride to town!"

"Yes you do," said Sally. "Remember, the doctor hasn't cleared you to start work again. Have you been doing your exercises?"

"Certainly," I said, "I don't have anythin' else to do."

The reunion between the five old timers went on that evening during and after supper. The weekenders were enjoying listening to the tales swapped between those guys. I thought I ought to be entertaining them a little, but they seemed to enjoy listening to the conversation. I was content to sit with Ginny on my lap and listen myself. Soon Ginny fell asleep and Sally took her to bed.

There were a few more guests than we'd had the previous week, so Sally asked Jimmy to accompany Ginny and her on the ride the next morning. It had stopped snowing, but there was about two inches of snow on the ground. It was cold, but the sun was out and it was warming up. For the guests' sake, Sally decided to wait until it

126

warmed up a little, then leave on the ride. There were a few guests that didn't know if they wanted to ride as cold as it was.

When it had warmed up and Sally was ready to leave on the ride, she informed those guests that had opted not to go that Pat could take them out later whenever they wanted to go. Ginny, Sally, and Jimmy took the ride out. They had eight riders and were planning on a two-hour ride.

Missus Abercrombie indicated she might like to go for a ride a little later. Pat saddled her horse and topped him off while she was in the lodge. He hadn't been ridden for a few weeks and Pat didn't want any surprises. He humped up a little, and after about fifteen minutes of being ridden, Pat was satisfied he'd be okay.

Around eleven o'clock, Missus Abercrombie indicated she was ready to ride. She told Pat, "I'd like to take Dusty out and show him the ranch."

"But, Virginia," said Mud, "Pat's already shown me a good deal of it."

"Mister Waters," said Missus Abercrombie rather curtly, "I would like to take you and show you the ranch!"

"Yes, ma'am," said Mud, somewhat meekly. He got his horse and Pat got Missus Abercrombie's horse.

"Would you like me to go along?" asked Pat

"Yes!" said Mud.

"No!" said Missus Abercrombie.

They left, with Missus Abercrombie in the lead and Mud following, reluctantly. Pat watched them leave and chuckled, "There might be some sparks that fly," he said.

It was obvious to me that Missus Abercrombie and Mud had known each other in the past. Just how well, I had no idea, but was curious about it. I asked Pat and he just said, "Yep, they used to know each other. Pretty well, in fact. But I'll let them tell you about it."

It was clear I wasn't going to get any information from Pat, so I decided I'd just listen. When the proper time came, I'd ask them about it.

The weekend went by and Sunday afternoon the guests left.

Sally and Ginny made their preparations to leave. Before they left, Sally asked Missus Abercrombie, "Are you coming to town with us?"

"No," replied Missus Abercrombie, "I'd like to stay on the ranch a little longer."

As Sally got in the car, she said, "Remember, Honey, I'll be out on Thursday to take you to town."

Jimmy's parents left. George had offered to help with the roundup, but he was only available on weekends.

Bud thanked him and said, "With Jimmy, Pat, Mud, and Sally, we should be all right. It might mean a little more riding, but we'll manage. By the way, give this to your wife. It's for the jams and jellies." He handed a check to George and although George didn't want to take it, Bud insisted. Very few people lost even a minor argument with Bud.

The week passed slowly—without anything to do, I missed Sally and Ginny even more. Missus Abercrombie and Mud went riding every day and I didn't find out anything about their past. I was still curious about them, but didn't ask. Mud appeared to be reluctant to ride with Missus Abercrombie, and he spent a lot of time thinking up excuses why he shouldn't go. But Missus Abercrombie was very strong-willed and Mud ended up going every time.

Thursday came and Sally ended up getting to the ranch early. "We need to hurry back. Nobody's at the house and I need to pick up Ginny," she said, as she rushed me to the car.

On the way to town, I asked Sally about Missus Abercrombie and Mud.

"I don't know the whole story," said Sally. "From what I heard, they were about to be married when Mister Abercrombie showed up. According to Daddy, he was a city slicker, really handsome and a smooth talker. Apparently he swept Missus Abercrombie off her feet and they got married. Just left Dusty Waters out in the cold.

"Daddy says that Mister Abercrombie was a no good gambler and a heavy drinker. He drank himself to death. After he died, Missus Abercrombie would come out here every summer. He left her quite a bit of money, his family was quite wealthy. She lived back East in the winter, only thirty or forty miles from where I went to school. She lined up Daddy so I could go to school there. I used to think she came out here every summer looking for her first love."

"Kind of a ranch romance, huh?" I asked.

"Yes," answered Sally. "It looks like she finally found him!"

"He don't seem too happy about it," I said.

"I think Mud was hurt pretty badly when she left him for the bum she married. That could be a reason why he became a hermit, I don't know. Missus Abercrombie doesn't talk about it much and Daddy says even less."

"They've been out ridin' every day since she got here," I said. "Mud doesn't seem too anxious to go."

"She might be making her amends or apologies to him," said Sally.

We picked up Ginny as school let out and I took them out to supper. While we were eating, I told Ginny, "I get to see the doctor tomorrow and if he says it's all right, would you like to take me out for a ride?"

"Oh, no, Daddy!" she answered.

"No?" I asked, "Why not?"

"You might fall off again!" I almost choked at her comment.

The next day the doctor released me for, as he put it, "light duty."

"What does that mean?"

"No heavy lifting," replied the doctor.

"That'll be easy," I said.

"How's that?"

"I've never been able to lift anything heavy!"

We got back to the ranch as Missus Abercrombie was signing in some weekenders. Our weekends were busy and that was good. It added more to an already positive cash flow.

I joined Ginny and Sally on their ride Saturday afternoon. Pat had my horse, Roman, saddled and I thought that was strange.

"I took the liberty of topping him off for you," said Pat. "He did crow hop a little, but nothing serious."

"I guess I appreciate it," I said, "but it wasn't necessary."

I got on Roman and he walked out, a little gingerly at first, but he soon lined out. I felt that he enjoyed getting out just as much as I did.

The weekend passed quickly. Late Sunday afternoon we had another visitor. Bud's brother, Rod, came riding into the yard, leading a packhorse and another horse. Pat saw him ride in before anyone else saw him. I recognized the horse he was riding, I'd broke him some years before.

"What brings you out this way?" asked Pat.

"I heard Honey was laid up, so I come to help out with the cow gather," said Rod.

"That's good," said Pat. "Many hands make light work. Bud's up at the lodge, he'll be glad to see you. He'll probably have you stay in the house. Take your bedroll up there."

Rod unsaddled his horse and unpacked his packhorse. He turned them in with the saddle horses, grabbed his bedroll, and started toward the lodge.

I accompanied Rod up to the lodge. Rod entered the porch just as Sally and Ginny were leaving to return to town. "Uncle Rod! It's good to see you, but we can't visit. We have to get back to town so Ginny can go to school."

Rod reached down and patted Ginny's head, much the same as he would pet one of his sheepdog's head.

"I understand," said Rod. "Drive careful!"

I gave Ginny and Sally each a kiss and they left.

Sale Day

Bud was glad to see his brother. It had been a year or two since they'd had a chance to visit. Bud came out on the porch and they brought each other up to date on what they'd been doing. When they were satisfied they had filled each other in sufficiently, Bud asked Rod, "Do you remember Dusty Waters, 'Mud' we called him?"

"Vaguely," replied Rod.

It was apparent to me that Rod hadn't run much with the old timers that were assembled at the ranch. At supper, Bud reintroduced Mud to Rod.

After supper, Bud announced the plans for the following day. "We'll run in the mares and yearlings we want to sell. A couple of days of handling will gentle them down and maybe they'll remember what we taught them earlier. We'll sort off the two-year-olds we want to sell and give them a little extra riding."

"They won't need much ridin'," I said. "They've been used quite a bit this summer. But a little tuneup won't hurt 'em."

"Good," said Bud. Turning to me he said, "Do you remember what dude horses we wanted to sell? We'll need to sort them from the saddle horses and give them some extra riding also. As soon as the horse sale is over, we'll start gathering cattle."

"The dude horses will be ready," I said.

Again Bud said, "Good!"

"You goin' to help run the horses in?" Pat asked me.

"I figured on it," I said.

"What horse you going to ride?"

"I'll probably ride Drygulch," I said. "He ain't been ridden for a while an' probably can use the exercise."

Pat just nodded his head and didn't say anything.

The next morning, Pat, Jimmy, Rod, and Mud ran the saddle horses in. I didn't help them, as they didn't keep a jingle horse in for me. I sat in the kitchen and had another cup of coffee and watched. When they came up for breakfast, Pat wasn't with them.

I asked, "Where's Pat?"

"He'll be up directly," said Jimmy, "said something about changing horses."

Pat came to the kitchen while we were eating, didn't say anything, sat down and started eating.

When we went to the barn, I found my horse, Drygulch, already saddled. "What's goin' on?" I asked.

"I topped him off for you," said Pat. "He's ready to go."

"You didn't have to," I said.

"Well, Sally asked me to."

"You don't need to go do extra for me," I said.

"I know," said Pat, "but it's done."

"I guess I appreciate it," I said.

We all mounted and headed out to where we'd put the sale mares and yearlings. We rode to the far end of the pasture they were in. I sent Pat and Mud to the southwest. I told Pat to hold everything they had at the gate, we'd take 'em all in together.

Jimmy, Rod, and I went to the southeast. We had the larger circle to make and there were a lot of draws and swales to check. I thought it would take about an hour to ride the pasture and there were enough of us that we could cover it thoroughly.

We came across a small bunch of yearlings and I sent Jimmy to start them toward the ranch. "Stay with 'em all the way," I said. "Rod an' I will check the rest of the pasture. Don't push 'em too fast, we need to catch up. Pat an' Mud will be waitin' at the gate."

We separated and Rod and I went to look for more horses. It felt good to be back in the saddle, even though it was kind of cold.

We found a small bunch of mares and their colts in a draw, and I sent Rod after them.

"Just follow 'em down that draw," I said. "You should meet up with Jimmy when you get out of the draw. I'll check the far corner an' meet you at the gate."

Rod nodded and started the mares and colts down the draw. I rode to the far corner of the pasture and started back toward the gate. I hadn't found any horses. *That'll be a heck of a note—the boss went out to look for horses an' couldn't find any! He came in empty-handed,* I thought. However, I was content that there weren't any horses hidden away in any of the draws that I checked.

Soon I met up with Jimmy and Rod. They were taking their time moving the horses toward the gate.

"Didn't find anything, huh?" asked Rod.

"Nope," I said.

"I picked up a couple more pairs farther down the draw."

"Good. Pat an' Mud will have the rest of 'em," I said.

We met Pat and Mud at the gate. They were holding the horses they'd gathered there. A quick count assured me we had all the horses we'd turned into that pasture.

"Pat," I said, "you an' Rod lead 'em home. Take 'em kinda slow, we ain't in no rush. Jimmy, Mud, an' me will follow."

I wanted Mud in the rear. I wasn't sure how well he could handle a stiff trot back to the ranch with his artificial leg.

They led out and Jimmy, Mud, and I slowly pushed the horses behind Pat and Rod. We made it to the ranch without incident about dinnertime and corralled the horses.

"Let's eat," I said. "All this ridin' has made me hungry!"

"I don't know that you can eat," said Pat.

"How's that?"

Pat answered, "We went out to look for horses and you're the only one that didn't find any! Around here, we only reward good behavior!" Everyone laughed and we headed for the kitchen.

At dinner we discussed the afternoon's activities. We'd catch each horse, halter them and start brushing them down. The more we handled them, the easier they'd be to handle at our sale. About three o'clock, we'd turn the horses loose in the small pasture and give each one of the dude horses we'd decided to sell a ride. We'd repeat this procedure every day until the sale date.

That night, I called our farrier and asked him if he could come out and trim the sale horses' feet. I also told him we'd need our saddle horses reshod. "They'll probably be about three days' worth of work, maybe four," I said. "We'll put you up an' feed you if you can make it."

We agreed on a date when he'd show up. I was content that we were ready for our horse sale.

Bud had indicated that he'd received some phone calls from people interested in attending the sale and told them, "We can put you up. We won't charge you anything for room and board for one night if you buy something, but if you don't buy, we'll have to charge you for room and board. We'll only give you one night's room and board free. If you show up earlier or stay later, we'll have to charge you."

Most of the folks Bud talked to thought this was all right and some made room reservations right then. It was just like Bud, looking to make a little extra money where he could. I knew where Sally got her ideas about making more money.

We'd scheduled the sale for a weekend when we didn't have any dudes and were careful not to schedule any dudes for that weekend. We'd be plenty busy with our sale.

Two days before the sale day, an outfit from town showed up and put up a large tent. Inside they put up portable panels to make a sale ring and spread sawdust and shavings in the ring. They erected some portable bleachers for seats. An electrician showed up and we strung extension cords from the barn to the tent so we could have a microphone and loudspeaker for the auctioneer.

When the tent was completed, we spent a lot of time leading the horses into the sale ring to get them accustomed to the place. Jimmy played some wild music over the loudspeaker system to get the horses used to the noise we expected. We even rode the dude horses we were going to sell through the ring. I was content we were ready.

The auctioneer showed up and provided us with numbers and

paste to stick on the rump of each horse to identify it. This was important, important enough that Sally took Ginny out of school for a few days so she could make sure it was done correctly.

Our sale day arrived. We had decided on our sale procedure. We'd sell the yearlings first, with each colt being led into the sale ring. Sally would sit by the auctioneer and give a description of each horse, its pedigree, and any other information about the horse she thought was necessary. She wouldn't have to act as secretary, as the auction company would provide its own. She would be consigned to remain with the auctioneer all during the sale.

After the yearlings were sold, we'd sell the mares and their colts. If necessary, we'd split them and sell them separately if someone only wanted a mare or the colt. The colts were old enough to be weaned. We'd sell the mares as "exposed" and not guaranteeing their pregnancy. And, of course, registration papers, breeder's certificates, and transfer papers were available. The brand inspector was there to provide the necessary brand papers.

Once the mares were sold, we'd take a break for the noon meal, at a cost to the people, of course. The cook was preparing a barbeque. The cost would be nominal and Missus Abercrombie would be in charge of the food sales. Rachel would help Missus Abercrombie.

After dinner, we'd sell the dude horses. They'd be ridden through the ring. I wanted Ginny to ride as many through as she could, just to show how gentle the horses were. We had Mud ride a few dude horses through the ring and Sally would point out that a one-legged man was riding this horse. When the dude horses were sold, we'd sell the two-year-olds as started ranch horses. Pat or I would ride the two-year-olds through the ring. Jimmy, Rod, and Mud would saddle and unsaddle the horses so Pat and I would always have a saddled horse ready to ride through the ring. That would complete our sale.

Our sale started and it was progressing well. Occasionally I would see Bud visiting with some prospective buyers. He was visiting, but also keeping track of each horse's status in the ring. He seemed overall pleased.

At the noon break, I asked him, "Are you pleased with the way things are goin'?"

"Pretty much," he said. "I was surprised at how much some of the yearlings brought and a little disappointed that some didn't bring as much as I'd hoped they would. Maybe these people know something I don't."

After the break, the sale resumed. The auctioneer took his time when the dude horses went through, he made sure each horse stayed in the ring a long time. When he started the bidding, he wouldn't back down. He knew his business. Even though the dude horses we were selling had some age, they still had a few good years in them. Every now and then I'd see Bud smiling broadly. I knew the horse that had just sold had brought more money than Bud figured. On the other hand, when a horse didn't bring as much as he thought the horse should have, I could see him telling Ginny, "That's too good a horse to sell that cheap. That guy got a good buy!"

By the time the sale was over, all the hands were tired, including myself. When Missus Abercrombie finished with the barbeque, she set up a table and started checking out the buyers. She made sure to get driver's license numbers on all the checks. She'd sold enough at the noon meal that she could make change for the people that paid cash. Jimmy had to leave his saddling and unsaddling chores to get the horses that had been paid for so their new owners could take them home.

As soon as the last horse was sold, Sally left the sale ring and went to help Missus Abercrombie. Pat, Rod, and I started to help Jimmy bring out the horses that had been paid for. Mud wasn't much help during this part of our sale, his artificial leg prohibited him from walking very fast, but he did try. Ginny stayed out of the way with her grandpa, except when we had her ride some dude horses through the ring.

A few of the buyers had made arrangements to stay overnight and take their horses home the next day, and this made our chores a little easier. When the buyers that were leaving had left, it was well past suppertime. The folks that were staying overnight had been fed leftovers from the barbeque and shown to their sleeping accommodations.

We did the evening chores and went to the lodge for supper.

The cook was apologetic as he set leftover barbeque in front of us. "I just didn't have time to fix something different," he said.

"Don't worry, Cookie," I said. "We're all so tired we couldn't do any of your meals real justice! I think everyone here will agree, we just want a little something to eat, then we'll hit the sack."

Bud nodded in agreement. He said, "Sally, I want you to figure the total sales today and give me a figure after supper. Virginia, how much did you take in from the food sales?"

Missus Abercrombie gave Bud a slip of paper. "Here's the total," she said. "Sally has the money. We had to make change, but it's all there except for what you took."

"Good," said Bud. "Offhand, I would say our sale was a great success. I'll know better when Sally gives me her figures. Now, let's eat! We need to get the people's horses that are staying overnight loaded in the morning, then I think we can take the day off tomorrow. The next day, we'll start gathering cattle."

"But Daddy," said Sally, "I'll be in town with Ginny for school! I won't be able to help."

"Daughter," said Bud, "I'm aware of that. But I've been watching the weather the last few days and there's a big storm coming. You couldn't see it from inside the tent, but there was a change this afternoon. The storm will be here sooner than the television people think. I think it's important we get started as quick as we can."

"Sally," said Missus Abercrombie, "if you like, I can take Ginny to town and school tomorrow."

"Would you do that?"

"Why, yes, of course." Missus Abercrombie gave Mud a sly look and Mud looked relieved.

"That's settled then," said Sally. "We'll be sure to keep my horses in tomorrow. Daddy, I'll have your sale figures soon." Sally left the room and went to the office to use the calculator.

Before we went to bed, Bud, Sally, Pat, and I went over the figures Sally supplied. She said, "I've counted the cash, subtracted

Missus Abercrombie's food sales and added the checks. The totals agree, but we're ten dollars short on the total cash. And I can't find it."

"Don't worry, Daughter," said Bud, "I gave Ginny ten dollars from Missus Abercrombie's food money for riding the dude horses through the ring. It should balance out."

"You gave Ginny ten bucks? I swear, you're spoiling that child!" said Sally.

"That's what grandpas are for," said Bud smiling. "Our sale has been a bigger success this year than what I expected. I'm very pleased. There'll be a little bonus for everyone in their paychecks this month!"

Sleep came easy for everyone that night. As tired as we were from the day before, everyone was a little late getting up the next morning. We ran the saddle horses in and started for breakfast. The overnight horse buyers were up and after we ate, we caught their horses, got them loaded up and on their way. We finished up the morning chores, sorted off the saddle horses we wanted to use for the cattle roundup, and turned the rest of the saddle horses into a different pasture. We wouldn't be needing them until early spring.

Pat said, "We'll need to bring 'em in and pull their shoes."

"Yep," I said. "We'll do that when the farrier comes out to reset our ridin' horses' shoes."

I thought we had all our bases covered and was content. "I guess," I said, as we rode back to the barn, "we got the rest of the day off."

We got to the barn and turned our horses loose. We kept in fresh horses to jingle on the next day.

Pat, Jimmy, and Mud went to the bunkhouse and I thought they'd probably take a nap and catch up on some sleep. Rod went to his room in the lodge. Sally was helping Missus Abercrombie get ready to go to town and explaining to Ginny why she wasn't going with her.

Ginny was not taking it very well. I heard Sally saying, "Daddy and the boys need Mommy to help gather the cattle next week."

"But I can help!" exclaimed Ginny, almost to tears.

"It will be very cold," said Sally, "and Pumpkin couldn't stand all the riding you'd give him."

"He's tough. He could take it," said Ginny.

"But your dad and I are going to use four or five different horses. It would be very hard on Pumpkin. I'll bet he would rather stay in the nice warm barn than be out in the wind, snow, and cold."

"Do you think so, Mommy?"

"Yes. And I'll be going to town next Sunday with you."

"If you're sure, Mommy," said Ginny.

"I'm sure," Sally assured Ginny. "And when we go to town next week, I can help you spend that ten dollars Grandpa gave you."

"You don't have to help me," said the little girl. "I already know what I'm going to buy with it."

"What? A surprise for me?"

"No, Mommy. I'm going to buy Pumpkin and Pumpernickel some horse treats! I have enough money now."

"You mean you're going to buy your horses a surprise and nothing for your mom?"

I had to chuckle when I heard the interaction between my wife and daughter. I thought Sally could handle any situation in a positive manner.

Ranch Romances

Ginny and Missus Abercrombie were about ready to leave for town. She told Sally and Ginny she had to say goodbye to Dusty—she'd just be a minute. Sally grinned and carried Ginny's bag to the car. I made small talk with Sally and Ginny while they waited for Missus Abercrombie. Bud came down and waited with us.

About half an hour later, Missus Abercrombie came to the car. She looked perturbed and got in the car and slammed the door. "Men!" she said disgustedly. I kissed my daughter goodbye.

Bud, noticing Missus Abercrombie's condition said, "You drive careful Virginia. That's my only granddaughter you have with you!" He said it in a tone of voice that made Missus Abercrombie take notice. They left for town.

The next day we were all up early. We saddled our best horses. It had started to snow during the night and I thought there was probably three or four inches on the ground in the mountains.

"Let's load our horses in the trucks an' take the easy way to the gate," I said.

"I was going to suggest that," said Pat.

"Make sure everyone's got a raincoat," I said.

"Raincoat? It's snowing," said Jimmy, "we need snow coats!"

Everyone laughed, although each one of us knew it was going to be a cold, wet day. A little laughter would help make the day bearable.

"We've got six horses an' six riders," I said. "We can load the horses in the two-ton truck. Pat, you drive an' take Jimmy an' Rod with you. I'll take Sally in my truck. Mud, you might be more comfortable ridin' with Sally an' me."

"In the front or back?" Again, everyone laughed.

"Well, you just suit yourself," I said, still laughing.

We loaded the horses and Pat started out. I followed. We got away from the ranch about a mile when Sally asked, "It's none of my business, but what's going on between you and Missus Abercrombie? You seem to be a little uptight when she's around."

"A little uptight? I'm downright scared. If I'd have known she was still here, I probably wouldn't have come up here to help."

"You knew she'd been here in the past?" queried Sally.

"Yes," said Mud. "That's why I didn't want to come visit your dad and Pat all these years. I would have come in the winter, when she was back East, but it was generally too cold and too far. I wouldn't come in the summer because I knew she was here."

"How come?"

"You've probably noticed she's a strong-willed woman, used to gettin' her own way. And she's bossy. Likes to boss people around. I don't like that," said Mud.

"You mean you don't like me because I'm the boss?" I asked, teasing.

"No, Honey, you're all right. I don't mind taking orders from you, you know what you're doin'. You got a head on your shoulders."

"I didn't ask you that fishin' for compliments," I said. "I was only jokin'."

"Jokin' or not, I mean it. But Virginia is different. Did you see the way she started bossin' me around? And we hadn't seen each other for twenty, maybe twenty-five years. You don't know how close I came to just ridin' off in the middle of the night. And I would have, but I told Bud and Honey I came up to help with the gather."

"And we appreciate it," said Sally.

"The last few days," continued Mud, "she changed her tune, became real sweet and almost likeable, like she wanted to pick up where we left off. Did you see the look she gave me when she volunteered to go to town with your daughter? I think she only volunteered to go because I told her she made me nervous. She might have been doin' me more of a favor than you, Sally. And pick up where we left off; as I recall, where we left off, she was married to that Abercrombie bum. "

"Daddy says he wasn't any good," said Sally.

"All he was good for was dying and leaving Virginia all that money," said Mud. "I certainly couldn't have done that much for her, I don't have anything, never had much anyways.

"I've got a nice little place now. Course it's a mess, but I'm comfortable in it. I've got a nice little garden and I can grow all I need. Don't know that I could grow enough to take care of two year-round."

"You mean she wants to move down there with you?" asked Sally, incredulously.

"She has said she'd like to come down and visit, to see how I'm doin' and livin'. I don't think I want her to come down. If she got there, it might be too hard to get rid of her. No," continued Mud, "it's easier to keep on just like we were, with her thinking I'm dead, only now she knows I'm alive. It'll be pretty rough from here on out."

Sally asked, "Is there anything I can say to make things better? We're pretty close. She's almost been like a mother to me. She said she would die trying to make a lady out of me, and I think she feels like she failed."

"She didn't fail," interrupted Mud, "I think she did a good job. That might be the only good thing I could say about her."

"Then there's nothing I can say or do to make things right between you two?" asked Sally.

"You might tell her to just leave me alone," said Mud.

"I couldn't do that," said Sally. "It might break her heart. There's a reason she's stayed around here so long and now I think I know why."

As I listened, it appeared to me that Sally might not be able to fix this situation. But they continued the discussion.

Mud asked, "What's the reason?"

"You," answered Sally. "I think she has been secretly hoping you'd come back to her."

"That's ridiculous," said Mud. "You've been reading too many Ranch Romance magazines!"

It was snowing harder now and I needed to use the windshield wipers to see where I was going.

"That might have been so some years ago," replied Sally. "I really believed those stories when I was younger, but I'm older now and I can see Missus Abercrombie's thinking. Right here and now, we're living in a real ranch romance!"

"Nonsense!" retorted Mud. "That's the silliest thing I ever heard. After all these years, she hasn't been waiting for me!"

"As you said, she's a strong-willed woman," said Sally. "She might be bossy, but since Honey showed up, she's mellowed some. I think Honey had a lot to do with that."

I was surprised. I hadn't had much to do with the old gal and was content to let her do her own thing.

"How did Honey change that old biddy?" Mud asked.

"As Daddy told me," said Sally, "Honey showed up when they were driving a bunch of cows and calves they'd gathered to brand. Daddy and Honey were following and Missus Abercrombie was up in the middle of the cow herd, following one cow, like a lot of the dudes do. Honey yelled at her, telling her to get out of the middle of those cows and added something like, 'it's hard enough driving the cattle without having to drive you too!' Missus Abercrombie was so shocked at being yelled at, she did what Honey said. Daddy said it was all he could do to stay in the saddle, he was laughing so hard!"

"Good for you, Honey," said Mud. "I knew you had a head on your shoulders! How come you call her Missus Abercrombie rather than Virginia?"

"When she came to stay with us after her husband died, Daddy told me that she was a lady of high social position back East. He said to call her Missus Abercrombie to show her respect. I started doing that and she never has said to call her anything different."

"Just like the old biddy," said Mud. "She's been trying to control people all her life. She wants all the respect she can get and demands it. You're an adult now, call her Virginia and see what happens. She won't do anything."

"I wouldn't dare," replied Sally. "Besides that, she has done a lot for this ranch over the years."

"Really?" said Mud. "It's hard for me to imagine her doin' anythin' nice for anybody at any time."

"She has. She's loaned Daddy money when he needed it and has helped me clean up cabins and train the maid staff in the spring. And she's quite helpful with Ginny."

We got to the gate where we needed to start riding for cows. Pat had backed the two-ton truck up to an embankment and was unloading horses when we arrived.

"Looks like it's time to quit ranch romances an' start gatherin' cattle," I said, as I turned off the truck and got out. The wind was cold and quite a contrast to the warm cab of the truck.

Everyone put on their raincoats. Everybody, except Jimmy, had untied their raincoat from behind their saddle and spread it out over their saddle to keep the snow off the saddle.

Jimmy brushed the snow off his saddle. "You learn something new every day," he said.

We checked our cinches and mounted our horses.

Jimmy added when he got in the saddle, "That's cold and wet!"

We all laughed as we started out. When we were through the gate, I started to send the riders off in various directions with instructions as to where to meet when they had some cattle. I finished by saying, "I'll take the big circle an' meet you all back here. Whoever shows up here first needs to stay at the gate an' count cows as they go through it." I closed the gate so no cattle could slip through without being counted.

"That sounds good," said Pat, "but you better let Rod, Jimmy, and me take the big circles. You ought to take a smaller circle and get back here first to get a good count on the cattle."

That made sense to me and I modified my instructions to accommodate Pat's plan. It didn't occur to me until later that Pat had devised his plan to make it easier on me because of my shoulder, easier on Sally because of her pregnancy, and easier on Mud because of his artificial leg.

Pat, Rod, and Jimmy started out at a fast trot. Sally and Mud went off to the east just as fast. I headed west, content to stay fairly close to the gate and keep an eye on it. I found a few cows and started them back toward the gate. I figured I'd have to come back and check on them just to make sure they made it. There weren't any cows with different markings that I could use as "marker cows."

I'd been gone about an hour and found more cattle. I started them toward where I'd found the first bunch of cows. They started meandering toward the gate, grazing a little as they went. I figured they would join the other cattle I found about half a mile from the gate.

I made a circle around the cattle and got to the gate, opened it and waited for the cattle to arrive. It had snowed another two inches or so since I'd left the gate and I figured there was about eight or nine inches on the ground. I got cold waiting for the cattle and wished they'd hurry so I could go to the truck and wait with the heater on.

The cattle arrived and I got a good count on them. Thirty-nine. I wrote it down. I started toward the truck when I saw Sally following a bunch of cattle heading for the gate. She was having a problem with a couple of cows that didn't want to stay with the rest. Satisfied that the cows I'd counted through the gate wouldn't return, I started toward Sally, making a big circle around her cattle so I wouldn't push them back on her. I'd started off in the direction of the cattle that were giving her a problem. When I got to the bunch of quitting cows, Sally went back to the bigger bunch of cattle she'd gathered and brought them in.

I pushed the bunch of quitting cows through the gate at a run and went back to help Sally. I got ahead of the cattle and counted them through the gate. Sally had gathered forty-four including the quitters. I wrote it down and added it to my figures.

"We can wait in the truck until we see more cattle comin'," I said. "Turn it on an' it'll be warm. Where's Mud?"

"I haven't seen him since we split up."

Sally gave me her raincoat and the reins to her horse, got in the truck and turned it on. I tied the horses to the truck, put the raincoats over the saddles and got in on the passenger side. "It's plenty cold out there," I said.

"Yes," shivered Sally. "I learned a lot coming out here. My suspicions were confirmed."

"You mean about Missus Abercrombie?"

"Yes," replied Sally. "I wasn't sure until I listened to Mud."

"I don't know that I'd try an' fix that," I cautioned Sally. "It sounds like to me that enough damage has been done already. Any more attempts to make things as they were might make things worse."

"But I feel sorry for both of them," said Sally. "They both seem so lonely."

"They've done all right to this point, I'd let sleeping dogs lie," I said.

Sally was quiet, contemplating the situation. I could tell she was giving it some serious thought.

Soon, I saw some cows coming over the low ridge south of us. "That'll be Mud comin' behind those cattle," I said. "I'll get my horse an' see if I can give him a hand," I continued. "You count the cows through the gate. You ought to be able to do that on foot. I'll slip up an' slow 'em down if need be."

I got around Mud's cattle and helped him push them toward the gate. When we had the biggest part of them through the gate, Mud rode over to me and said, "Pat, Jimmy, and Rod are about a mile and a half, maybe two behind me. "They've got more than a hundred head. I'll ride back and give 'em a hand."

"That's a good idea," I said, "but why don't you follow these cattle through the gate. Sally's got the truck's runnin' an' it's warm inside. You've been out in the cold all day, get inside an' warm up. I've had a chance to get warm."

"Well," said Mud, "my artificial leg has been gettin' cold. It's steel, you know."

"Go to the truck an' warm up. Don't push the cows too fast, Sally's countin' 'em."

Mud seemed relieved that he'd have a chance to warm up, and I felt kinda good that I could spell him in this gather. I rode toward where I figured the cows would be coming from and when I saw them, I made a wide circle around them so I wouldn't turn any of them back. I saw Jimmy on the far side of the cattle, Rod was behind the main herd, and Pat was pushing a bunch from my side of the main herd. I had to widen my circle so I wouldn't push any cattle back on Pat.

"What are you doin' out in weather like this? It's not fit for man or beast," said Pat, trying to joke.

"I'm out enjoying the day an' lookin' for some cowboys an' cows I thought might be lost," I said.

"Well, you found us," said Pat. "If you're enjoying this there must be somethin' wrong with you! We're doin' all right here, you must really like this to want to help."

"Partner," I said, "I ain't enjoyin' this any more than you, but it's got to be done. The gate ain't far away. We'll put these through the gate then head for the ranch. We can call it a day."

"Did you get many cattle?"

"I got thirty-nine an' Sally got forty-four," I said. "Don't know what Mud got, Sally's countin' them through the gate."

"Mud all right?"

"He appears to be. He said he was goin' to come back to help you, but I convinced him to follow the cows through the gate. He did say his artificial leg was gettin' cold."

"He'd have come if you let him," said Pat. "He's a tough old codger. That truck heater will feel good goin' home."

We pushed the cattle toward the gate. I saw Sally get out of the truck as the cows approached. She went to the two-ton truck and started it, then took up her position by the gate where she could count cows. Rod rode closer to her so he could slow the cattle down if they got to coming too fast. Mud stayed in the truck.

When the last cow went through the gate, we followed. I closed the gate and asked Sally how many cows she'd counted.

"Mud brought in fifty-one," she said. "This last bunch numbered one hundred and twenty-one, if my count is right."

I added the figures. "Two hundred fifty-five, not even half of the cow herd. This gather is goin' to take us a little longer than I counted on."

"I think," said Pat, "that the cattle have drifted east with the storm. We'll probably find more tomorrow when we ride that direction."

"I hope so," I said.

We loaded the horses in the two-ton truck and headed toward the ranch. It had continued to snow all day and I guessed there was about a foot and a half on the ground at the gate.

Sally was strangely quiet on the ride home and didn't pursue her conversation with Mud. I thought she'd either taken my advice to let sleeping dogs lie, or was busy thinking up a way she could play matchmaker. I hoped she'd decided to let the situation resolve itself.

When we reached the ranch house, there was only about ten inches on the ground. As we unloaded the horses, I told everyone, "Grain your horse good tonight. We'll need to keep our horses in so we've got jingle horses in the mornin'. We'll need fresh horses tomorrow an' these horses have earned a good feed today."

After we took care of the horses, we went to the lodge for supper. Bud and the cook met us. "Was it cold out there today, boys?" Bud was joking.

"Colder than a mother-in-law's kiss," answered Mud. Mud was the last one in the lodge and when he entered, I noticed a limp on him that was more pronounced than it had been before.

"Come in," said the cook. "I've got good, hot beef stew for supper and it'll stick to your ribs. And there's plenty."

It didn't take long for everyone to get washed up and start eating.

During supper, I filled Bud in on how many cows we'd gathered and where we'd ridden. He didn't look disappointed. "That's not bad," he said. "Not for this kind of weather. I'd suggest you take a day off tomorrow. I've been listening to the weather and this storm is not going to end until day after tomorrow. Your gather might be more successful when the storm breaks."

"We could do that," I said. "We probably ought to load up some hay an' take it to the cattle we gathered today. They'll work their way home, but the snow has covered most of the feed. Once we start feedin', we'll need to keep it up. The cows will stop huntin' for their feed."

"If we take a load of feed out to the cattle, they'll follow it home," said Pat.

"That's what the plan is for tomorrow," I said. "I'll take a horse out an' hurry the cattle along behind the truck."

"You start out while we're loading the hay," said Pat. "I understand you're not supposed to lift anything heavy."

"We can do that," I said. "If things work out right, we can have the cattle on their feed ground by the end of the day."

The next day went as planned. I got awful cold moving the cattle toward the feed ground. Around noon, Sally brought out a thermos of coffee and a sandwich. I appreciated that, the coffee warmed me up some.

As I ate the sandwich, I asked Sally, "What did you decide?"

"Decide about what?"

"You were very quiet on the way home yesterday," I said. "I think you were contemplatin' your next move in the ranch romances, ah ... saga, is that the right word to use?"

"You think you can read me like a book, don't you?" stated Sally.

I smiled. "It's gettin' easier," I said.

"Well, smarty, I haven't decided anything ... yet. I'm still thinking about it."

I finished the sandwich and stuck the half-full thermos of coffee in my saddlebag. Sally went back to the ranch.

I got to where Pat and Jimmy were feeding and offered them what was left of the coffee. They drank it and Pat said, "We'll be done here shortly. We can put the rear tires in a ditch and jump your horse in the truck, if you want."

"No thanks," I said, "you're liable to get the truck stuck. I'll just ride back."

The next day we gathered our saddle horses, saddled them, loaded them in the two-ton truck and headed out to make another roundup.

Jimmy rode out in my one-ton truck with Sally and me. He said it was at Mud's request—Mud felt like he'd talked too much when he rode out with Sally and me earlier.

I laughed. "Mud is on to your scheming, Darlin'," I said.

Sally didn't say anything. Jimmy wondered what was going on and I explained the situation briefly to him.

The storm had pretty well broken up and we only had a few snow flurries during the day. I sent the riders off in different directions, making sure that Mud and Sally got a short circle and I got the big circle. It was cold even when the sun came out.

We gathered a lot of cattle that day. Sally brought the cows she found back first and got a count on them. She counted the cattle Mud brought when he showed up. They sat in the truck until the rest of the riders showed up. I'd found quite a few cows and mixed them with the cattle Pat found. Rod and Jimmy brought their cattle. When the day was over, we'd gathered over five hundred head of cattle, more than twice what we'd found two days before. I felt good about that, I thought the previous gather was somewhat of a failure.

I asked everybody, "Are you all okay? It's tough goin' out there." They all answered that nothing had gone wrong. "We'll let the cows wander home," I continued, "an' bring out some hay tomorrow, just like we did yesterday. That seemed to work good. Then, we'll hunt more cows day after tomorrow. Let's load up an' call it a day. It'll be dark when we get back." I was glad to call it a day. It had been bitterly cold.

When we got back to the ranch, I noticed Mud's limp was more pronounced than it had been. "Are you okay, old timer?" I asked.

"Yep," said Mud, "never better."

"You seem to have a bigger hitch in your git-along today."

"That's just the weather," he said. "It's worse in cold weather."

The next day we proceeded like I'd outlined and the day went well. I'd checked our numbers against the count of the cows we'd turned out after each branding. We were still short about forty head.

I was discussing this with Pat, and he said, "We're out more than that. I saw six of the neighbor's cows mixed in with ours. They might have some of our cattle, but I doubt they've got forty head."

"I'll call 'em tonight an' tell 'em what we've got. We'll take 'em down to 'em an' if they've got any of ours, we can pick 'em up.

We'll have to ride that country again. It would be nice if we could gather everything in one day!"

"We'll never do that," said Pat. "We've got too many cattle an' too much ground to cover. Course the good thing about that is it keeps old cowboys employed."

I laughed. "Yep," I agreed, "although I wonder if that's a benefit as cold as it's been. I'm sure there's a lot of hands that would prefer to be unemployed rather than work in this kind of weather." Pat agreed.

"Missus Abercrombie will be out tomorrow, weather permittin'. Do you think Mud will duck an' run? She's been puttin' a lot of pressure on him. I got some of the story the other day. She makes him mighty uncomfortable."

"He won't run," said Pat. "He's not that kind. He'll be here until after the cow sale."

"That's good," I said, "but do you think he can take this hard ridin'? I've tried to put him on the short circles an' he still comes in like he's been halfway beat to death."

"My guess is that he can take it," replied Pat. "He did say that if he'd have known Virginia was here, he wouldn't have showed up in the first place."

"I heard that from him the other day."

"He won't leave until Bud or you says our gather is over. Bud offered him a job through the winter, but he won't take it. Especially since Virginia's here."

You know," I said, "after our cow sale, we still have to run in the broodmare bunch an' wean the colts. Can we use him for that?"

"I think so," replied Pat. "He's still a good hand and knows both cattle and horses."

Later that night, I called the neighbors about their cattle we had. They said they had eight of our cows and volunteered to bring them to our ranch. Turnabout is fair play, as I'd delivered their cows to them the year before. They indicated that they hadn't completed their gather, they were still missing some cows. I told them we were in the same boat and we agreed to exchange cattle when we had completed our gathers.

The next day we rode the country again, finding about half our missing cattle. We decided to start sorting cows and calves and preg checking the cows. The vet had shown up with an assistant to preg check the cows and they would stay in a cabin until the job was done. The cold weather would bring the rest of the cattle down and our cow sale date was approaching. While we were riding, Missus Abercrombie and Ginny showed up at the ranch. She had a stranger with her.

"This young man," she told Bud and Sally, "is looking for work. He's not a cowboy, but he says he can do ranch jobs. He answered the ad in the paper. I brought him out to talk to you. I said he could stay at the ranch over the weekend. If you hire him, he has a job. If not, he could ride back to town with Sally Sunday night. His stuff is in the back of the car."

The young man's name was Clark Summerhays. Bud and Sally talked to him explaining what the job would be, mostly helping to feed during the winter. Bud told him that we'd use him for a week and if he worked out, he'd stay. If not, we'd give him a week's wages and a ride back to town. Jimmy showed him where he could bunk in the bunkhouse.

Sally asked me if I wanted to talk to him.

"No," I said. "If he's good enough for you and Bud, he's good enough for me."

Seeing that Virginia was there at supper, Mud was a little reluctant to come in and eat and when he did, he took a seat at the table as far away from Missus Abercrombie as he could get. The discussion at supper was mostly about the gather and the upcoming cow sale. We would proceed much the same as previous years, providing meals and a place to stay for the buyers and charging those who didn't buy.

The next day, Pat, Rod, Mud, and I sorted the calves from the cows. We turned the cows out and sorted the steers from the heifers in the afternoon. We had enough hands that we could sort the longhorn calves from the rest at the same time. It was easy to tell the longhorns, they were all sorts of colors. They made up a colorful bunch of calves. While we were sorting cattle, Jimmy and Clark loaded hay and fed the cows. Then they loaded hay to feed the calves. The vet and his assistant had a day to rest before they started their chore. With our calf sorting chores done, we made ready to preg check the cows.

The following day, Pat, Rod, and Mud kept the chutes full for the vets as they preg checked each cow. The open cows were sorted off in a separate pen. Mud ran the gate to the open pen, as there wasn't as much walking in that job.

While the hands were doing the preg checking, Sally and I decided to saddle up and go look for more cattle. We loaded the horses in my truck and went to where we had made our first gather. We'd closed the gate when we left and when we got there, we found a few cows and their calves wanting to come home. We unloaded the horses and went through the gate, leaving it open so the cows could start toward the feed grounds.

"We'll need to take the cows an' calves all the way to the ranch so we can sort the calves an' get the cows preg checked," I said. "When we get back, load your horse an' go ahead of the cows, openin' the gates. I'll follow the cows an' close the gates when I come through."

Sally nodded her head. It was too cold to talk and she had her face pretty well covered. I sent Sally on a small circle and I made a larger circle. Sally found a few pairs and started them to the gate. I didn't find anything and when I got to the gate, I found Sally sitting in a warm truck, her horse already loaded. I got off my horse, tied him to the truck, and got in the cab to warm up.

"I thought I better wait for you," said Sally, "just in case you needed some help. The cows that were here have started home, and I let the pairs I found start. You sit here and get warm. I think it's gotten colder since we started and we have plenty of time."

"You're the boss," I said. I appreciated the warm truck. I sat in the cab for about half an hour and didn't want to leave.

"Load your horse, cowboy," said Sally. "We can follow the cows back in the truck and you can stay warm."

"I like your thinkin', Darlin'. I'll be glad to do just that! If the cows an' calves mix with those that have been preg checked an' turned out, we'll just come out an' get 'em tomorrow."

153

We had a stroke of luck. The cattle that had already been pregnancy checked hadn't been turned out. We got all the way to the corrals without meeting any other cattle. We put the pairs in an empty corral.

Sally drove to the barn after she let me out. She unloaded the horses and started to unsaddle them. I hollered at her that I'd do that, but she just ignored me.

Jimmy and Clark had thrown off hay where the main cow herd was going to spend the night and were helping out with the preg checking. I told them to throw the pairs we brought some hay, "Enough to keep 'em overnight."

I went to take care of my horse, but Sally had already unsaddled hers and mine.

"You didn't have to do that, Darlin'," I said, "but I appreciate it."

"That's all right," said Sally. "It just needed to be done. I'm going to the lodge and check on Ginny."

"Fine," I said, "I'll see how the vets are doin'."

I met Pat at the corrals. "How's it goin'?"

"We're doin' just fine," said Pat. "Two more days and we'll be done."

"Good," I said. I noticed Missus Abercrombie standing in the corral where Mud was turning the open cows into. "What's she doin' here?"

"She came down to visit Mud. She brought some hot coffee for everyone, so I let her stay. Now that you're back, I'll turn out the pregnant cattle. I kept 'em in because I didn't want to mix anythin' you'd brought with 'em. The feedin' is done, we shouldn't have to worry about 'em."

"Is Missus Abercrombie causin' any problem?"

"No," answered Pat. "Other than she might be pestering Mud some. I ain't goin' to interfere with that situation, I'll let it work itself out."

"It's colder than it needs to be," I said. "I think I'll see if I can spell Mud for a little bit."

"Good luck," said Pat.

I started toward Mud and Missus Abercrombie. Pat followed and went past where Mud was. Remembering what Mud had said earlier, I said, "Virginia! Aren't you gettin' cold out here?"

Pat heard my comment, paused for a second, turned around, smiled and went to let the cows out.

Missus Abercrombie looked surprised when I called her by her first name. It took her a second to recover. By the tone of my voice, I think she figured it out that I wanted her to go to the lodge.

"I'll see you at supper, Dusty," she said coyly as she left. She didn't neglect to give me a dirty sneer.

I noticed it and said, "You'll certainly be more comfortable at the lodge."

When Virginia was out of hearing range, Mud said, "You sure saved my bacon, Honey! She had me trapped here and I couldn't leave."

I smiled at Virginia's sneer and Mud's comment. "That's only part of my job here," I said.

"Well, you do it real good, but you could do some of it sooner," said Mud.

I smiled again. "Sometimes the timing of my actions is a little off," I said. "Do you want to go to the lodge an' warm up?"

"With her up there? No, not until it's absolutely necessary! If I could eat in the bunkhouse tonight, I'd do it!"

"You really don't like to be around her, do you?"

"No, I don't," answered Mud.

"Why don't you just tell her where to go?"

"I was raised to be a gentleman," replied Mud. "If I told her where I think she needs to go, she'd be offended. I figured I'd just wait it out, leave and never see her again. I really don't want to hurt her feelings, but I'll be glad when this job is done."

"Mud," I said, "that's confusin' to me. On the one hand you say you don't want to be around her an' on the other, you say you don't want to hurt her feelings. I don't understand it."

"I know," said Mud, "that's the hard part of bein' a gentleman!"

"Mud, you slip up to that room by the chute. There's a heater in there, you go up an' get warm," I said.

"I know," said Mud, "Pat's been givin' each of us a spell and we go there to get warm. I'll go. Last time Pat wanted me to go, I didn't. I knew Virginia would follow me. I'd rather be cold and move around here some."

"You're really afraid of her, ain't you?"

"Of course," replied Mud. "What if she got me alone and got my artificial leg? I'd never get away from her, one-legged like that! I don't even have a set of crutches here!"

I laughed and sent Mud to the warming room and operated the open pen gate.

Before Mud got back, Pat came to me and said. "We're goin' to call it a day. The vets are gettin' tired and it won't be long before it's dark. Jimmy and Clark are feedin' the cattle that haven't been checked and they'll feed these open cows. We're about done."

"Good," I said. "It's really gettin' cold out here."

I went to the barn and found Sally and Ginny feeding Pumpernickel. "Is everythin' all right here?"

"Yes, Daddy. Isn't Jimmy doing a good job of taking care of Pumpernickel?"

"You bet he is, Ginny. It's gettin' colder down here, let's go to the house and get warm. Say good night to your horse," I said.

Ginny did as she was told and we went to the lodge to get cleaned up for supper.

Escape

The next afternoon, Sally and Ginny went to town. Sally had stayed longer than she'd intended and Ginny had missed some school. Sally said it was necessary.

Missus Abercrombie had decided to stay at the ranch, much to Mud's dismay. Feigning being tired, he went to the bunkhouse right after supper. Missus Abercrombie started to follow him, but Bud stopped her by saying, "Better let him go, Virginia. He's pretty tired. He's had to do double the work of the others, he's only got one leg, you know." Bud chuckled at his comment.

Virginia gave him a strange look, but didn't follow Mud.

I felt a little sorry for Missus Abercrombie. She wasn't getting what she wanted with regards to Mud and she seemed to be losing her status at the ranch.

The next two days were busy checking the cattle. About three in the afternoon, we were done. The vets got showers and gave their bill to Bud.

"I'll call Sally and have her bring you a check while she's in town. You should get it tomorrow afternoon."

"Don't forget to deduct the room and board," said one of the vets. "You forgot to do it last year."

"I didn't forget," said Bud. "That was on me last year and this year also."

The vets said, "Thanks," and left.

The feeding for the day got done, the evening chores were done. We were done early that day. With the vets gone and Sally and Ginny in town, there was plenty of room at the supper table, but Mud continued to sit as far away as he could. Mud continued to act tired or pretend his artificial leg was giving him problems and left for the bunkhouse right after supper every night. Clark would generally leave when Mud left.

The cow sale was coming up. Pat, Rod, Mud, and I continued to ride looking for missing cattle. Jimmy and Clark did the feeding every day. At noon, Jimmy would harness a team and feed with them. He alternated the teams on Bud's advice. The teams hadn't been used all summer and Bud advised him to start them out slowly to get them in shape.

One night after supper, Jimmy asked to talk to Bud privately. They went into the office and closed the door.

"Bud," said Jimmy, "I hate to be the bearer of bad news, but I don't think Clark is going to work out."

"How come?" asked Bud. "Isn't he working?"

"Oh, he's working all right. In fact he's a good worker."

"What's wrong then?"

"When we thought he was going to the bunkhouse with Mud, he was really going behind the barn and smoking," said Jimmy. "I followed him the other night."

Bud chuckled. "What's wrong with that? As you know, a lot of our dudes smoke."

"Marijuana?"

Bud's attitude suddenly changed from jovial to serious. "Are you sure?"

"Yes, I'm sure," replied Jimmy.

"How do you know?"

"Bud," said Jimmy, "I used to smoke the stuff and even sold it. That's part of the reason why I was on probation when you first brought me out here."

"I'll need more evidence before I take any action," said Bud. "Tell Honey and Pat to come in here and don't mention this to anybody."

Jimmy left Bud in the office and told Pat and me he wanted to see us.

158

We went into the office and found Bud in a very serious mood. He got right to the point. "Jimmy tells me that Clark has been smoking marijuana out behind the barn each night when he follows Mud after supper. I want you two to follow him tomorrow night and verify this accusation."

"I don't think Jimmy would lie about somethin' like that," said Pat. "In fact, I don't think Jimmy would lie about anythin'."

"I don't either," said Bud, "I trust him completely. But I need more evidence before I take any action." Then, remembering that he had turned the ranch and its operation over to Sally and me, he swiftly added, "Before *we* take any action. Right, Honey?"

"That's right," I said, smiling. I never took offense when Bud took the reins and control of the ranch, even though he had entrusted me with it. I liked the way he handled things.

"But if he's been smokin' that weird tobacco, we need to let him go," I said. "It's against the law."

"We need to give him a chance," said Bud. "Follow him tomorrow night. If he's smoking that stuff, bring him up here. Don't say anything to anybody else about this."

The next day, Pat, Rod, Mud, and I sorted off what heifers we wanted for replacements. We also sorted the longhorn steers from the heifers. Now we were ready for the cow sale.

That night after supper, about a minute after Clark followed Mud to the bunkhouse, Pat and I followed Clark. Jimmy was right, Clark went to the side of the barn, rolled himself a smoke and lit it. Pat and I both saw the match light as he lit his smoke.

"What's goin' on here, Clark?" I demanded.

"Just thought I'd have an after supper smoke," said Clark, as he went to put it out.

"You don't have to put it out," said Pat.

"Better come up to the lodge with us," I said. "We need to discuss this."

Clark followed me to the lodge and Pat followed Clark. He took another puff from his smoke and flipped the unsmoked portion into the snow as we approached the lodge. Unbeknownst to Clark, Pat picked up the butt before we entered the lodge.

Jimmy and Bud were sitting at the table. Bud motioned to the office as we entered the lodge and the three of us entered the office. Bud followed and closed the door.

"It has come to my attention that you have been smoking marijuana down by the barn each night," said Bud. "Is this true and what do you have to say for yourself?"

"It's true I've been smoking down by the barn," said Clark. "But not marijuana."

"Then what's this?" said Pat, holding the unused portion of Clark's smoke.

"I roll my own," said Clark.

"Really?" I asked. "Where's your makin's?"

Clark reached in his pocket and pulled out a sack labeled "Bull Durham."

Pat took it and looked at it. "This isn't Bull. I used to smoke it and this doesn't look or smell like Bull at all."

I looked at Pat in surprise. I never knew he smoked.

"Bull Durham is just the sweepings off the floor," he continued. "I even heard somebody opened a sack one time and found a dead mouse in it. Does this look like Bull to you Bud?" He handed the sack to Bud.

Bud looked over the contents of the sack. "This doesn't look anything like I remember Bull looking like or smelling like, and I've smoked a lot of it in the past, too. What do you want to do, Honey?"

I asked Bud, "Did you ask him if he used drugs when you talked to him before you hired him?"

"Certainly, you know that's part of our interview process."

"What was his answer?"

"He told me he didn't use drugs," replied Bud.

"He lied to you then," I said. "And he tried to pull the wool over our eyes just now. I don't think he can be trusted here and we need to let him go."

"That settles it then," said Bud. "Clark, get your things and put them in Honey's truck. I'll pay you cash for your time and Honey can take you to town. You're done here! We have a good reputation to protect and one hand can ruin it. Pat, you go help him get his things together. Here's your pay." Bud paid him on the spot.

Pat went with Clark. I knew Bud didn't send Pat to help Clark, he sent him to make sure Clark didn't take anything that wasn't his.

"Honey," said Bud, "you take him to town and let him off at a motel. Take Jimmy with you, he can stay at his folks. I'll call them. I'll call Sally and tell her you're coming. You and Jimmy can come back tomorrow."

"I don't need Jimmy," I said.

"Yes you do. Clark's probably not very happy about being fired. He might slug you, or worse, and steal the truck. With Jimmy along, he probably won't try anything."

"I see your thinkin'," I said. "I'll get Jimmy."

Clark had gathered up his things and I told him to put them in the back of the truck.

"Why not the front?" asked Clark.

"Jimmy's goin' with us," I said, "he wants to see his folks."

"It's about time," said Jimmy.

The ride to town was quiet. Clark started to roll another smoke and I stopped him. "If you're goin' to smoke that in here, you can ride in the back," I said, as I slowed the truck and started to pull off the road. It was cold and Clark thought about it and put his stuff away.

I left Clark and his things at a motel, waited until he got checked in, then drove Jimmy to his folks.

I told him, "I'll call before I come to get you. You might be able to sleep in some in the mornin'."

"I doubt it. I've gotten used to getting up early," he said.

I drove to the house Sally had built in town. The lights were on, Sally was waiting for me.

"Daddy called me. Clark didn't work out," she said.

"Nope."

"That's too bad, he seemed like a nice guy."

"I think Bud was concerned about our reputation," I said. "Anyways, it's better for everyone if we don't have any potheads around."

"I had pulled our help wanted ad," said Sally. "I'll put it back in tomorrow."

"Yep, we'll need to hire more help for the winter. I'll go by the employment office in the mornin' on the way to pick up Jimmy an' head back to the ranch. I guess Pat an' Rod will feed. Jimmy and Clark loaded the hay when they got done feedin' today. Is Ginny still up?"

"No. She's been asleep for hours."

"What time is it?"

"It's after midnight," said Sally. "Come to bed and get a good night's rest."

"You shouldn't have waited up," I said.

"That's just part of my job," said Sally with a smile and a kiss.

I'd had a good visit with Ginny during breakfast the next morning. After Sally took her to school, I went by the employment office on the way to pick up Jimmy and relisted our open position with them. I added that we needed two people. And, I added no potheads or druggies need apply.

As I left the employment office, I saw Clark entering. "Need more help?" he asked.

I didn't bother to reply.

I picked up Jimmy and we drove back to the ranch. On the way, Jimmy apologized for reporting on Clark.

"There's no need for that," I said. "You did the right thing. We'll find more help."

When we got back to the ranch, Pat, Rod, and Mud were feeding with one of the teams.

"Looks like we got back just in time to load hay for tomorrow's feeding," I said.

"Yep," answered Jimmy. "It's a good thing I'm here. It would take those three old timers all day to load the wagon."

"You might be interested to know that I've asked the employment office for two men," I said. "You'll be goin' back to school after the first of the year an' that just leaves Pat an' me. Mud's goin' back to his place an' Rod's got his sheep to look after."

"It's nice to know that I'll be replaced by two men," said Jimmy, chuckling.

"I don't think you realize how valuable you are to this outfit," I said.

We waited for the three old timers to come in for the noon meal, then ate. After eating, Bud wouldn't let me go out and help load hay. According to him, we had to discuss our hired help situation. I figured it was a ploy to keep me from lifting too much on account of my shoulder.

There wasn't much we could do about the help situation until someone showed up, but Bud kept me busy until the hay was loaded and our hands came to the lodge. Our conversation was mostly about how apologetic Virginia was about bringing Clark out to the ranch.

"What are your plans for tomorrow?" asked Bud.

"I thought after we got done feedin', we'd gather the broodmare bunch an' wean the colts. It might be good advertisement to have a bunch of colts standin' around durin' our cow sale. Somebody might see one that he likes an' buy him."

"Good idea," said Bud. "Pat an' Mud can help you run in the mares, if we can get Rod and Jimmy to feed."

The next morning, Pat, Mud, and I saddled our horses and went after the broodmare bunch. They weren't hard to find. Pat and I led the bunch in and Mud followed. When we had the mares corralled, Mud came up and said, "That looks like a good bunch of colts."

"Yep," said Pat. "That stud you shot threw some good ones. We don't know what this younger stud will produce in the future, but he had some good colts last year."

"You know," said Mud, "I only shot that stud to put him out of his misery."

"I know," said Pat.

"You also know that I'm leaving after the cow sale," stated Mud. He said it in a matter of fact manner that left no room for discussion.

"I've heard rumors to that effect," replied Pat.

"I can't say that this has been the most pleasant couple of weeks I've ever spent. I've been mighty uncomfortable with Virginia pesterin' me the way she has. It's been kinda nice to ride with you again and to visit with Bud. And that Honey, he's all right. But Virginia, well, she sure puts a damper on things when I'm around."

Pat just smiled and said, "I understand."

"I need to slip away when she's not around, and get back to my place without her knowing," said Mud.

"You mean escape?" asked Pat, halfway laughing at Mud.

"That's exactly right," replied Mud. "I do feel like a prisoner when she's around."

"I think it's against the law to help escaped prisoners," said Pat. He was having a good time joking with Mud.

"This ain't no laughing matter," said Mud. "This is almost a case of life or death. Leastways, it affects my well-being."

I was listening to this conversation from a distance, and enjoying it.

"You mean," Pat asked, "you'd ride off into the sunset and leave that poor woman crying all alone, mourning her loss just like in the old time movies?"

"In a minute," replied Mud, "and I'd be smiling all the way home."

It was clear that Mud had made up his mind and no one was going to convince him differently.

"You know, it's a long ride to your place from here," said Pat. "It would probably take you two days, long days at that."

"I know," said Mud. "I rode up here, remember? Besides, my horses are well rested now."

"You suit yourself," said Pat. "But remember, Bud has offered you a year-round job here."

"I know, but I'll be more comfortable at my place."

We sorted the colts from the mares and took the mares to another pasture where they'd be easy to feed during the winter. It was closer to the barn.

As we rode back to the barn, Pat said, "You know, we could

use a lot of help halter breakin' the colts this winter. You used to be pretty good with the young horses."

"Ain't interested," replied Mud.

It was clear to me that Bud had put Pat up to trying to get Mud to stay. But Pat wasn't having any luck. Mud was as stubborn as a Missouri mule.

We got back to the barn, took care of our horses, and went to the lodge for coffee.

Pat, Bud, and I went into the office for a little conference.

Pat told Bud, "I tried, but couldn't convince him. He's figurin' on leaving, escaping, he calls it, when Virginia isn't around. Riding off into the sunset." Pat smiled when he said that.

"That's a long ride down to his place," said Bud. "It'll break Virginia's heart, but we better help him get home when he wants to leave. It's too cold for him to ride. Do what you have to Pat. Honey, after the cow sale and after the feeding is done, when Rod wants to leave, load up his horses and give him a ride home. We'll be stuck here, but we'll manage somehow. Maybe Rod and Mud won't want to leave on the same day. That'll help some. It'll be just you, Pat, and Jimmy until we get more help."

When we exited the office, Missus Abercrombie was sitting next to Mud, talking at him. Mud looked very uncomfortable and appeared to be paying attention. However, I suspected that what Virginia was saying just went in one ear and out the other. As we approached, Virginia, lowered her tone and her final words were, "And you remember that, Mister Dusty Waters!"

Rod and Jimmy came in from feeding for the noon meal.

Virginia left Mud and we all sat down to eat, with Missus Abercrombie seated at the far end of the table. It was a very quiet noon hour.

"Day after tomorrow is our cow sale," said Bud. "Some of our buyers should start showing up tomorrow. Rachel, are the cabins ready?"

"Yes," answered Rachel, "and I've even prepared a few extra ones. Last year, some of the truck drivers stayed over and didn't load up until morning."

"Good," said Bud. "Sally will be out tomorrow night. She'll act as my secretary, just as she's done in the past. Virginia, you can give Sally a hand and keep an eye on Ginny. Rachel, you can help keep an eye on Ginny and give the cook a hand when he needs it. Jimmy, if you and Rod will feed early, we'll have that out of the way. Then you two can help Honey, Pat, and Mud accompany the buyers into the corrals after you've eaten. When they want to make a bid on something, bring them to me. We'll sell the heifer calves first, then the steers, then the longhorn crosses, heifers first then steers. After that we'll sell the cull cows then the cull bulls. It might take us two days, depending on how long the buyers spend in the corrals. They'll probably want to cut off some, so have your horses saddled so you can sort off what they don't want out of each bunch. We'll make those they cut back available to whoever wants them.

"Tomorrow, after the feeding, just hang around and take it easy. You might make yourselves available to help the buyers get settled in their cabins, just like we do with the dudes. Any questions?"

Jimmy asked, "What about the weaner colts?"

"We won't worry about them until later, when we have more help. We'll just keep them in the corral for a few days for now."

The next day, a few buyers showed up and after we had helped them get settled, they visited with Bud. Their discussion was mostly about the cow business and how low the cow prices were. I thought this was mostly to set Bud up to accepting lower prices for his cattle, but Bud had been in touch with some sale yards and was aware of what the prices were.

Sally showed up that evening with Ginny. We were all set for the next day.

The next morning, Jimmy and Rod fed early, before the sun was all the way up. They came in late for breakfast. The rest of us were already at the corrals conducting business. Our sale was going smoothly and Bud seemed pleased with the offers he was getting. By noon, we'd sold all the calves. We broke for the noon meal and after dinner, we sold the cull cows and bulls.

Some of the buyers came to the lodge to use the phone to call for their trucks to come. Trucks had already started arriving to haul the successful calf buyer's cattle out. The afternoon was spent loading calves onto trucks. Bud knew a lot of the buyers and frequently he would ask them if they knew of anybody looking for work. The buyers' answer would generally be, "I don't know of anybody, but will keep my ears open and send them to you if I hear of someone."

I noticed this and thought it might be more effective than our newspaper ad. Word of mouth advertising generally produces good results.

During the night, a few more trucks arrived and those drivers spent the night in their trucks.

We spent most of the next day loading cattle in big semi rigs. It was a long day and I was glad we'd saddled our horses to move cattle around in the pens, alleys, and up the chutes to the trucks.

Bud watched the procedure from outside the loading chute. "I'm sure glad I plowed the snow away from the yard here and that the ground is frozen," he said. "We'd really have a mess here if I hadn't."

"Yeah," I said, "look at the alleyways. They've been chewed up pretty bad. It's tough goin' for the horses an' a lot of mud is showin' up." I pointed to my chaps, already covered in mud and cow manure. Bud just smiled.

When the last bull had been loaded and the last truck pulled away, we could relax. All the buyers had left.

"Are you satisfied with the sale?" asked Pat.

"I think so," said Bud. "Prices were off a little compared to last year, but I think we did all right. Some of the guys tried to get me on shrink, but I wouldn't give in. Those cattle will shrink enough being trucked."

"I think Mud will pull out early in the morning," said Pat.

"I'll talk to him tonight after supper," said Bud. "I'll offer him a job again. It probably won't do any good, but I'll try. And I need to pay him for his work. If he's dead set about going, you load up his horses in the two-ton and take him home. I don't know what else we can do to try and keep him. I'll see when Rod wants to leave and have Honey take him home. Then, I think our most important chore is to find more help. It'll be really tough on you and Honey this winter after Jimmy leaves if we don't find more help."

After supper, Bud and Mud went into the office alone. They were in there a long time. Sally, Missus Abercrombie, Rod, and I waited in the front room by the fire. Pat and Jimmy had gone to the bunkhouse.

Missus Abercrombie asked, "Do you think he's asking Mud to stay?"

"I'm certain of it," I said. "I don't think he'll have any luck, Mud's pretty hard-headed."

"You can say that again!" said Missus Abercrombie. "Heaven knows I've tried!"

"Maybe you tried too hard," volunteered Sally.

"That may be," replied the older woman, "but I didn't know what else to do. He is awfully stubborn."

"What will you do if he decides to go?" I asked.

"There's nothing I can do," she replied. "Once he makes up his mind, he's set."

Mud left the office and Bud wheeled himself out behind him, shaking his head negatively. I could see Bud wasn't successful. Mud said goodnight to everyone and went to the bunkhouse.

Missus Abercrombie asked Bud, "Did you do any good? You were in there a long time."

"I'm afraid not, Virginia. He's pretty set on leaving. I spent most of the time trying to get him to accept the pay I offered him. I finally got him to take it by threatening to break his other leg. He said he'd leave in the morning."

"Well, at least I can say goodbye then," said Missus Abercrombie. With that, she left the room and went to her quarters.

"I feel so sorry for her," said Sally. "She's really a nice lady. And so lonely."

"Lonely?" I asked.

"Yes," said Sally. "We've talked. A lot."

"Don't fret over it, Daughter. What happened, happened a long time ago and some wounds take a long time to heal."

Around four in the morning, I heard the truck start up. I figured Pat was taking Mud home.

At breakfast that morning, Missus Abercrombie noticed that Pat and Mud weren't present. "Where's Mud? And Pat?" she quickly added.

"I heard them leave about four this morning," I said.

"He snuck away, just like a thief in the night," said Missus Abercrombie.

I thought I could see a tear or two well up in the old lady's eyes, but she fought them off. "Oh well," she said. She picked at her breakfast and soon said, "I'm not very hungry. I think I'll go to my room."

Seeing she was visibly upset, Sally got up to follow her and lend some consolation.

"Best leave her alone, Daughter," said Bud. "She'll probably have a good cry then be all right."

Sally thought about it and decided to follow her father's advice.

Later that afternoon, Pat returned.

"How was your trip?" I asked.

"According to Mud, we made his escape positive. He was smiling all the way to his place. The most I'd seen him smile all the time he's been here. I tried to tease him about riding off into the sunset, but he wouldn't have any of it. In his words, 'The sun wasn't even up yet. We made a clean getaway!'

"His so called escape was successful. He did admonish me not to bring Virginia down to his place and not to tell her where it was. And he told me to tell you that also, Honey. I never saw a man so afraid of a woman!"

Other Books by Stu Campbell

Horsing Around a Lot

Horsing Around the Dudes

Humor Around Horses

You Can't Be Serious!

Comedy Around the Corral

More Humor Around Horses

A Young Cowboy's Adventure

Honey

Surprise!

Intruders

Expectations

Frozen

Advice

Broken